1

A Head of the Game

An Alaskan Serial Killer Novel
By
Rosalyn Stowell

I can do all things through Christ who strengthens me.
Philippians 4:13

Cover photo by Rosalyn Stowell Photo of the author by Samantha Stowell. Thanks to Kara Stowell for proof reading, any remaining mistakes are my own.

Other books by Rosalyn Stowell
Don't Use A Chainsaw In The Kitchen – How-to and Cookbook
PAW (Post-Apocalyptic World) Trilogy
The Beginning – Book 1
The Dark of Night – Book 2
The Dawn – Book 3
Alaskan Gold – novel, romance
Alaskan Alibi – novel, suspense
Stikine – novel, suspense
Cold Gold – novel, suspense
Klondike – novel, historical
A Head Of The Game – novel, suspense, serial killer

Chapter 1

Driving out of town this time of year was gorgeous and the fact that the four men were going hunting made it even better. The trees were at the peak of autumn colors, the hills golden with reds and crimsons showing through as accents just often enough to relieve the scene of monotony.

Even though they planned for this all year long and knew exactly where they would go and what they would do, it was still as exciting as the first time they made this trip.

Hunting was their excuse, but they really did not care that much about whether or not they actually got anything, it was the being out in the wilderness of Alaska, north of Fairbanks that drew them. Plus, it gave them a wonderful reason to buy the great toys they were pulling on the trailer behind the large crewcab pickup, 4 wheel drive, of course. These boys loved their toys.

"Hey, Jer, I read in the paper that you are thinking about running for State Legislature. Really? Politics?" "Pudge" Alistair McCrea asked.

"Well, you know what they say about believing what you read in the papers."

"Aw, come on, you would be great at the job and we do need someone that actually has some common sense down there in Juneau." George Lacey spoke up.

"The truth is, I'm done thinking about it and have the papers filled out to file to run, when we get back to town. I wanted this last bit of peace and quiet without worrying about a reporter jumping out from under a rock somewhere with a camera, recording me taking a dump in the woods."

"Yeah, that would jump start your campaign alright." And the whole group joined in the laughter.

Jerry Cameron, Jer to his friends, drove on while the rest teased him about his intentions once he got into office. George wanted to know if he planned on getting some cute Interns, Pudge smacked him and told him to behave or he wouldn't get introduced to them when they went and visited down in Juneau.

"Aww, come on fellas, I haven't even filed yet and you have me elected and with Interns even. C'mon this is me we are talking about. I don't have the best track record in the dating field, so why would I hire young women when I really do want to make a difference down in Juneau and try to help straighten out the State finances. IF I get elected, I want to hire the smartest, nerdiest kids in UAF to come work for me."

"Well, that is a step in the right direction, Jer. Maybe I will even vote for you." Terrence Markham, known as Marky, spoke up. Since they usually disagreed on anything political, this was quite an endorsement from his friend.

"Are you sure? Don't want you getting into trouble for actually being FOR me on this." Jer answered.

They all laughed and continued on their way, stopping at the truck stop for the last really good meal they probably would have, the rest of the trip. Pudge even going so far as to getting a second meal in a to-go carton and a pie on the side.

"How you can eat like that and never gain a pound is beyond me, you have to have a tape worm or something. What do you weigh, anyway, maybe a hundred pounds?"

"I weigh the perfect weight for someone that is 5'11" tall."

"Yeah, except you are 6' 5""

"Details, details. Besides, if you ask nicely, I planned on sharing the pie. If you remember right, George said he was cooking tonight, so you might want to order yourself another meal to go, also."

By the time they were ready to leave, they each had another to-go container, including George.

"Hey, I just remembered what my plan was for dinner tonight and we are doing it, right now."

"Wow, best meal you've ever fixed, George, and thanks, Buddy, I wasn't expecting you to pay for 2 meals each for us."

"I was hoping that would get me off the hook for cooking for a while, this trip."

"Well, maybe. After all, none of us can top this, anyway."

When they arrived at the spot they had decided on, they were pleased to see no one else camping there already. It gave them access to the White Mountains trail, kept their vehicles off the main road and a secluded area to camp. There was even a small stream nearby for water to wash up in and do dishes. George was really thinking ahead, he brought paper plates enough to last a month or two, no running out on this trip. There were plastic utensils, also, but the best were the individual knife, fork, spoon sets so each was responsible for their own, each even engraved with their nicknames on them. No getting them mixed up on this trip. Everyone remembered the year they forgot plates and eating utensils and had to eat out of the pot everything was cooked in. They even carved out wooden spoons so they at least didn't have to share that. They were best of friends, but there are limits.

They turned their vehicle around so they could park the trailer and pull away, yet have easy access to hooking it up again, in case anyone else pulled in, also. Setting up was simple, they had done it so often, and they knew just how they liked it done. The tents went in a semi-circle beyond the trailer, the kitchen area over to one side, and large stones rolled into position for a bonfire pit. They had hauled those stones in here a few years ago, and would roll them back out of the way, yet again, when they packed up to leave again, this year.

Yup, this was going to be a trip to remember.

Chapter 2
1 month earlier

He was so pleased with himself he could almost shout it out to the world. Not only had he managed to come up for parole and get it, he found the joys of the internet while in prison and had a whole new identity waiting for him when he got out and disappeared. He even managed to put his own fingerprints on his new ID. Did they really think they could still keep him under their control now that he was a free man?

Getting a job out here in his old stomping grounds was pure luck. His new identity had impeccable credentials. Shaving several years off his age and a bottle of hair dye worked wonders. Few would recognize him and probably no one would, since he had been gone almost 20 years. They would pay, they would ALL pay.

He had started, on a small scale already. There had been fires under suspicious circumstances in the homes of some of the people that had sent him away. It did not matter that some of the actual people were already dead, their kin still lived there.

He used to spend as much time as possible on the internet, researching the people he planned on retaliating against and if necessary, their entire families. After all, he used to be quite the arsonist.

Recently, he hacked into the system and listed himself as deceased, then deleted his release records. Then he did laugh.

He was in great physical condition, thanks to the health care and dental attention received in prison. He never had let himself go to seed. Yes, he could be considered old now, but he was in far better shape than a lot of men half his age.

He already successfully restarted his old hobby of picking up hitchhikers. The first one was a bit disappointing. She was no sport at all. Girls used to have more spirit to them, even if they were taught to submit rather than fight. These seemed to be too docile for much fun and games. Maybe he would have to think up new variations.

He was loving the new digital technology. He had a nice camera and tripod set up so he could record the proceedings and view later. He spotted several flaws in his technique and was working on perfecting them. It took time and patience to reach perfection. He had both.

If he got it right, he might consider posting to the internet, anonymously, of course. Public computers were a wonderful invention.

The girl waiting for him tonight would be in for a treat. He had some new ideas to try out and she at least had put up a fight. Futile, but she had fought. Oops, he better pay attention or he would be in danger of losing this plum job. It was so perfect, he couldn't believe it. He just had to stay alert.

At his house, the girl waited. She was tied to a bench and had no idea where she was. The ties were quite tight and she could not feel her hands or feet. The tape across her mouth made it necessary to breath carefully through her nose or she was in danger of panicking and choking herself. Her mind was racing and she knew she may never leave here alive. In fact, it was almost a certainty. She had seen him, he made no effort not to let her see his face. She had fought as hard as she knew how, so now her only weapon left was her mind. Would it be better if she complied with everything he wanted? Would it be better to continue fighting? She didn't want to die, but she also didn't want to suffer.

She continued to try to move her fingers and toes, hoping the blood was still getting to them even a little bit. Tears leaked under the tape across her eyes. That was going to hurt to be pulled off. Why had he bothered, since she already saw him? Was it just because he could and a type of sensory deprivation?

She was afraid to give in and really cry as the tape across her mouth would constrict her breathing enough even crying might choke her. She allowed the tears to fall, hoping to soak away some of the tape and kept licking at the tape on her mouth for the same reason, hoping to loosen it a bit.

She found by raising herself a little bit, she could work her hands underneath herself and bending down, pull them under her feet to place her hands in front of her and ease her aching shoulders a bit. Once her hands were in front, she rubbed the knots across the tape, hoping one or the other would loosen a bit.

She didn't know how long he would be gone. So she continued working on her bonds and by the tingling pain in her hands, realized she was making progress.

She had no way of telling how long it took her, but she managed to free herself of her bonds. She found a bathroom by crawling around the room. Her feet were too painful to stand on. As she was coming out of the bathroom, she heard a vehicle pull in by the house. It sounded like the one she came in yesterday, so she went back to the bench and sat back down, primly in the same position she had been left in, this morning, only no bonds on her, no tape.

As soon as he walked in the house, he knew he had made a mistake about this one. She was free. However, she had not ran away. Was this a sign? Was she to be of help to him? She sat quietly, calmly, as though she were at home. The pulse in her throat was beating frantically, but she gave no sign of fear.

He moved a small table over near her and sat a sandwich and soft drink he picked up on the way home, down for her. She didn't speak, which was in her favor, she looked at him inquiringly as though asking permission. He smiled and told her she was a good girl, go ahead and eat.

She smiled at him and daintily picked up the sandwich. She normally would not be so dainty, but her hands still hurt too bad to just grab the food and her mouth was sore from the tape, so she ate delicately, savoring each bite. She did not know if this was her last meal, so she would drag it out if she could.

The girl had class and good manners, maybe he would just keep her a while. He could pick up another one to practice on. There was always the shed out back, so this one would never know. He knew how to get sympathy and fool the establishment, how hard could it be to keep one small woman fooled?

Now he had to plan. He usually never let anyone run around in the house, they were usually confined, one way or another. He didn't want to carve on her and damage her yet. She was ingenious on getting untied. He thought she was tied so tight she would never use her hands or feet again.

His windows already had shutters fastened over them, and could only be opened from outside. His doors had key only deadbolts. He could probably just lock her in every day, there were no neighbors to hear if she screamed. He would hide all matches and lighters so she couldn't even burn the place down around herself to escape.

She listened to him muttering to himself, and realized he was figuring out how to keep her alive a while. She decided she would try to play along, and wait for her chance to escape. She realized he liked her dainty eating, so had to remember that. He also liked that she did not talk. One more thing to remember. She would have to study him and remember every little thing. She didn't think it would take much for him to change his mind about keeping her alive.

She thought being dead would be worse than being a temporary slave. She might change her mind, later, but right now, it looked better to her.

Chapter 3

Opening day of hunting season found Jerry, George, Pudge and Marky out on the White Mountain Trail on their 4 wheeled ATVs.

The scenery was gorgeous and they stopped to watch the sun rise over the White Mountains. There was no snow on them yet, but the limestone outcroppings looked white all year around, giving the mountains their name.

They took plenty of photos and talked of what they would like to do next year out here. They thought maybe they should come back out during the winter and do this by snow cat. They could rent one of the BLM cabins and stay overnight out on the trail. They would probably never do it, but it was fun to talk about.

They made their way, leisurely stopping whenever another photo op appeared as they traveled. It was a truly spectacular morning and riding the ridgetop trail with the Beaver Creek drainage below them on one side and first the Tatalina, then the Tolovana drainages on the other made it breath taking, indeed. There was enough glint of frost showing to add the sparkle of ice crystals on the low vegetation at the elevation they were traveling at to add interest to the pictures they were taking. There were only a few very stunted trees this high up and they did not obstruct the view at all. About 150 miles to the south, they could see Denali, majestic even at this distance. To drive there would be almost twice that far.

As they continued on, the sun stretched higher into the sky, but never coming directly overhead. There is never an overhead noonday sun up here, the sun circles the horizon. In summer, ducking behind the hills a few hours but never dark. More like the sun behind a cloud. In the winter, it briefly peaked over the southeastern horizon looped across a small arc and set in the southwestern sky, like an elongated sunrise/sunset combo lasting a very few hours. Lucky for residents, the sun is just below the horizon a few hours before and after sunrise and sunset, so there are several hours of half-light which is fine for working outdoors in. Not that so very many residents actually want to work outdoors in it all that much. Go play? Yes. Skiing, dog sledding, tobogganing, snow machining, it all was fun, and so had a lot of enthusiasts.

Right now, it was a deliciously perfect day. Just enough nip in the air to keep a good coat and hat on, but warm enough to not be burdened by so many layers of gear that it was hard to move.

They went by a lovely large bull moose, laying down over under some brush. He watched them go by, then stood and stretched, slowly, majestically, then he trotted down the hill into the White Mountains Recreation Area. Not a one of them had seen him. They were so intent on their progress and the scenery opening up ahead of them that no one was checking along beside them as they traveled.

By late afternoon, they had covered many miles without seeing a single moose. However, three legal bulls had seen them. None as close as the one this morning, but close enough.

They considered the day a great success and headed back for camp. They arrived just before dark and parked. Tonight was Marky's night to cook. He had planned his dinner with great care. He dragged a cooler out of his tent, after getting the fire started. Then he went into the woods, coming back out with several long thin poles. Opening the cooler, he yelled, "Come and get it."

There were assorted types of hot dogs and brats in the cooler, along with chilled beer. The bags of chips were set on the little folding table and mustard, ketchup and relish along with the buns were lined up beside them. Yes, dinner was ready, cook your own.

No one bothered with utensils or plates, so there were no dishes to clear away after dinner. Marky had planned on not having to spend time on KP duty. He seldom cooked at home, he saw no reason to cook on a fun trip. He had enough ice in the cooler and the nights were cold enough it should last, so he would probably repeat tonight's dinner on his next night to cook, also. He didn't mind eating the same thing more than once.

"Hey, Guys, what say next year, we take enough time off to stay out here the entire season?" Pudge asked. "We could maybe bring a couple of travel trailers or an RV if you think it might get too cold for comfort."

"I'll ask and see if I can get away the whole time. Usually some of the other guys like to go and the boss won't let more than one of us be gone at a time." George answered.

Jerry said he would have to see whether or not he got elected. He didn't think he could take off hunting season his first year in Office, if he was.

Marky said it would not be the same if they were not all along for the trip. He didn't think he could close up shop for the entire season, either.

"We better get some sleep, guys, morning will be here in a few hours and tomorrow, we are going to get one." So saying, George headed for bed.

Pudge pushed the glowing coals apart in the rock ring and everyone headed to their own tents. George was right, morning would soon be here.

Chapter 4

The girl was not one of his usual hobby projects. This one was very smart and such good manners. He was actually pleased with her and only had to reprimand her once for any infraction and she behaved perfectly after that. Of course he had never taken the time to get to know any of the others. This was the first time he had to interrupt what he was doing to go to work.

If he felt himself getting irritated about anything, he headed out to the shed in back and relieved his frustrations on the one staying in it. She was not going to last much longer. Oh well, he could always pick up another one.

The girl did not realize just how lucky she was. She had survived so far on mostly good luck and was afraid it would run out soon. She could see when he was getting angry and felt herself shrink inside, trying not to antagonize him. She was so afraid, that she didn't even consider not doing what he told her to do. She always breathed a sigh of relief when he left the house. She never dared fully relax as she felt like he could watch her, even when he was not there.

She searched carefully and finally did find a spycam up in a corner of the room. She was glad she had not openly searched. He seemed to get more upset when he thought she was opposing him in any way. She really didn't want to upset him.

***

When he reached the shed it was very quiet inside, not the usual scuffling sounds made when she heard him coming. When he opened the door and switched on the small inside light, he could see she was hunched over in a heap near the far wall. As he approached her, she moaned and slowly opened her eyes. The glazed look in them with no sign of recognition told him she probably wouldn't last the night. Oh well, she had been fun for a while. Tape still covered her mouth.

He spread a tarp out on the floor and proceeded to go to work. The sounds soon stopped.

***

On his way to work, he made one stop to dispose of the trash and another to finish his project. He would look for another project soon.

As he left the area, he noticed there were others around now, too. He had forgotten moose season. Oh well, it was no concern of his and he would not let it bother him.

He actually felt energized all day and thought maybe he would pick up the pace on his little projects. He hadn't even felt this good back in the day.

On his way home, he spotted a young woman at the edge of the road, but as he slowed down, a young man stepped out of the bushes beside her and they hugged. No, he didn't need a couple. It was better to pick one up at night, anyway. The later the

23

better. He had not had time to smear mud on his plates nor put on a disguise of any sort, either. This was best left alone for now.

He found he was anticipating opening the door to his house and finding the girl exactly where he told her to be before he left this morning. He knew she used the bathroom during the day, but she did not know exactly when he would walk in, so tried to stay as close to the bench as possible. He checked his spycam often, to make sure. If she did not behave, she could retire to the outside shed. He knew, sooner or later, she would end up out there, he just didn't know what would set himself off to actually go ahead and do it.

The power he felt having someone so completely at his mercy was overwhelming. He might have to see about keeping one around longer, more often. He felt this one would be the standard he would be looking for in every one of them, from now on. He thought it might be his version of love. He had to smile about that. Imagine that! Him, in love.

When he could stand the suspense no longer, he opened the door. When he walked into the room, she was sitting, right where she was supposed to be, posed exactly how he had told her to sit. He patted her on the head and walked back into the other room. If she was his pet, he should name her. He would think about that. He brought the bag of food in and sat it on the small table. He must not be bringing her enough food as she was visibly thinner than when he first got her. That wouldn't do, can't starve the pets. He would have Animal Rights groups after him and he laughed again.

This was seriously one weird man holding her captive. She never knew what made him chuckle once in a while as he watched her. It wasn't quite so bad when he talked to himself. He evidently didn't realize he did it and she could hear what he was saying. So far, she thought that was all that was keeping her alive. Some of the things he talked about chilled her blood.

She didn't know if he was serious on some of the things he said, but figured the fact that she was here as a prisoner, it was probably all true. If so, she was now living with a monster and it was doubtful if she would survive to tell about it.

He locked her in the large dog kennel at the foot of his bed for the night and threw the blanket over it. As beds went, it was not the most comfortable. But it sure beat being tied back up sitting on a hard bench all night. She would not dream of complaining.

He thought it was funny when he let her out in the morning to ask if she needed to go outside. Then he led her to the bathroom. "Take your time and a shower, if you want. I'll be right back with some doughnuts for breakfast."

When her eyes widened, he smiled and asked if she liked doughnuts? She nodded yes. "Okay, see you in a few minutes."

Yes, he was going to have to feed her a bit more. She was definitely getting skinny. Doughnuts ought to be a good start. Maybe name her Éclair or Rover.

When he returned, her hair was still damp from the shower and fell in long tangles down her back. He handed her a brush and comb to use while he set the doughnuts on the table.

As she worked the tangles out of her hair, he sat and watched her until he realized he needed to get going to get to work on time. He sat a jug of juice near the door before locking it, and left her to her juice and doughnuts.

It felt downright domestic to be getting things for someone else's comfort and meals. It would add a new dimension, making her project even more special, when the time came.

Chapter 5

The trip was progressing beautifully. The weather was holding perfect for them. Maybe not cold enough for actual good moose hunting, but great for them to enjoy themselves.

They had taken some small side trails off the main trail and found more beautiful scenery. This really was a perfect way to spend a week. They had even actually seen one of the many bulls they had passed over the days. This bull was very large and very far away, across a steep and deep canyon from their position, so none of them wanted to take a chance on shooting him. They did take pictures just to prove that they did go moose hunting and graduated to moose seeing.

Over the years, they had been accused of not even going hunting. Everyone in town thought maybe they actually got tickets and spent the week in Vegas. Anchorage, at the very least. They were almost insulted that anyone would think they preferred Anchorage to being out here in the wilderness. Now they took pictures with time date stamp on them and made a point of showing them around.

Jerry surprised them all by preparing a very nice meal on his night to cook. He started the night before and dug out a hole beside the campfire. That morning, he browned a nice roast in a Dutch Oven, then placed potatoes, onions, carrots and cabbage around it, and shoveled part of the fire over into the hole,. A shovel of dirt on top, then the Dutch oven, more coals from the fire and mounded the whole works with dirt before they left for the day.

While Pudge and Marky started the evening fire, Jerry dug out the Dutch oven very carefully and set it on the table. He brought out another Dutch oven and stuck it down in the hole and covered it back up. Then he carefully lifted the lid on the Dutch oven. The steam rising from the contents smelled wonderful and they soon were all filling plates, then stomachs. "Jer, when did you learn to cook?" asked George. "That is really good."

"I watched some outdoor show and they were talking about it, so I tried it in my backyard. The neighbors probably thought I was digging a grave back there."

Everyone sat back, patting their tummies. "That just might have been the best meal this trip." Pudge said.

"Oh, the meal isn't quite over." Jerry went back with the shovel and dug the second Dutch oven up. As he lifted the lid, the smell of hot fresh apple cake wafted out on the breeze. A can of whipped cream from his cooler to top it with on each plate made it a perfect dessert.

Pudge held his stomach and groaned. "I don't think I can hold another bite."

Jerry held out the spoon with the last piece of cake on it. Pudge dove for it before anyone else could even say "No thanks."

"Any of the whipped cream left?"

"Why yes, there is just a bit." And the can landed beside him.

"Ah, perfect."

"What time do you guys have to be home tomorrow?" Jerry asked.

"Any time, for me, not due back to work until the next day anyway." George said.

The other two agreed. No early start to town, just mosey along, taking their time and maybe, just maybe, they might get a moose on the way in.

The next morning, they took their time clearing up camp and reloading the pickup. The trailer was hitched up and the ATVs loaded. George was making a last check around the camp and stepped out into the woods to take a break when the others heard a choked yell.

They all headed over, a couple even grabbing guns just in case it was a bear or something that got George. When they could see him, he looked sick and was holding onto a small tree as though if he let go he would fall down. He could not speak, he only pointed.

When they looked, they lost breakfast, also. There was a large black plastic trash bag in the culvert mouth with a human hand sticking out. Through tears in the bag, more pieces of a person could be seen. Jerry unobtrusively clicked a few pictures, not wanting to seem ghoulish, but wanting to preserve evidence.

They hurried back to their vehicle and headed out to the main road. The Pump Station was just about a mile to the right, town was over an hour to the left.

A few vehicles went by as they sat and discussed what to do now.

They decided to go turn it in at the Pump Station so it could be taken care of as soon as possible. When they turned off the main road, they did not realize it is a bit of a drive to reach the Pump Station, but they were determined to get this reported, so continued on to the gate.

When they pulled up at the gate, a very official security guard came out, shrugging into his jacket and holding his roster to see what they wanted. His name tag simply said, Art.

"What's the matter? You guys look like you saw a ghost or something."

"We found a body back down the road and want to turn it in, here." Jerry said.

"You have it with you? Don't you know not to disturb a crime scene?" the guard asked.

"We didn't touch anything, we saw it, left it and came directly here."

"Oh, okay. I will need to take your information and go fill out some paperwork inside the shack there. Hand over your licenses and I will be right back with them." And the Guard held out his hand.

Everyone dug out licenses and handed them over. The Guard took them inside the shack. Through the window, they could see him on the phone to someone and he looked very official. They all breathed sighs of relief. It was out of their hands now, they could relax.

After writing down everything from their licenses, the Guard brought them back out and handed them over.

"Okay, let me get this straight. One more time. Exactly where did you find this body and what were you doing there?"

"You know the old road pullout, just on the left after leaving here, heading toward town? We have been camped back in there all this week. While cleaning up around camp and making sure we did not leave any mess, George happened to find a torn black trash bag like contractors use. The large heavy duty kind. It was stuffed into the mouth of an old culvert there and possibly an animal chewed into it or something, but there was a human hand sticking out and we could see more pieces through some other tears in the bag. We did not touch anything."

"Okay, I will give your information to the police. They will probably want to get in touch with you, since you are the ones that claim you found a body. You can turn your vehicle around right here. You are not allowed to proceed through the gate."

After back and forthing a few times, Jerry finally got the trailer turned in the cramped area. Once they were headed back toward town, Marky spoke up. "That Guard was sure Mr. Helpful, wasn't he? Right up there with really believing us, too. I think we need to also turn this in, when we reach town."

"I plan on it." Said Jerry.

32

"Why don't we just drive straight over to the Troopers and all go in?"

"Sounds like a plan to me. Guess we don't stop at the truck stop on our way home, this trip?"

"Somehow, I really don't have the appetite." They all agreed.

***

At the Trooper's office, they were not treated as badly. The Trooper assigned to talk to them was very professional and sounded like he believed them, especially when Jerry pulled out his camera and showed the pictures. Then Pudge pulled out his phone and showed what he had and so did George and Marky.

"Okay, I believe you. That definitely is a hand sticking out of the bag. I actually placed a call to an Officer that is out on the Elliott right now and he is headed over there. There is another one headed south from farther up and he will also pull in there and assist. I have sent a crime scene tech crew out, also."

"Thanks. The Guard at the Pump Station seemed to think we were practical jokers or worse, so it is nice to be believed."

"It's actually too bad you stopped over there. That is one more person that knows about this and he probably has spread it all over the Station by now. I just hope no one messes up the site." The Trooper told them.

"Sorry, we just thought he could call it in here faster than we could drive in and let you know."

33

"So far, there is no record of any phone calls coming in from the Pump Station."

***

The Trooper from town pulled in to the old road pullout and found the Guard from the Pump Station walking toward the road carrying a trash bag of old clothing and a car seat.

"What do we have here?" he asked the Guard.

"Did those idiots come bothering you in town, too? They pulled down into the Pump Station, swearing they found a bag with a body in it. I came on over before calling it in, since I don't want to be responsible for a false report. All I find is this bag of old clothes and a car seat. I don't know if this is their idea of a joke, or what, but I find it in poor taste." So saying, he threw the bag of trash into the back of the company pickup and got in. Starting it up, he told the Trooper, "I'm sorry you came all this way for nothing. Arrest them for false filing, if you can."

The Guard pulled out back toward work and the Trooper sat there a bit, wondering just what to do. About then, the crime tech crew pulled in, so they decided to look the area over, just in case the Guard had missed something. The crew had a copy of some of the pictures taken by the hunters, so they had more to go on.

When they reached the culvert, it was obvious the other bag was gone. However, there still might be evidence in the area, so they set to work. All the dirt that was under the bag, was picked up and bagged. They could see where the other bag had sat, so this was not difficult. They even picked up some of the bugs that were plentiful right there.

They fanned out, searching a grid around the area, stopping once in a while to bag and label something. By the time the second Trooper arrived, they were searching farther out from the original location.

As the Trooper walked over toward them, he spotted movement from the corner of his eye. When he turned to look, he saw the tail of a fox heading out through the woods. He marked the direction and told the other searchers and they started a grid in that direction.

Soon, they spotted the fox again. It seemed to be headed towards something, so they stayed back enough not to spook it and continued following. When they reached the den with the kits, they saw all the evidence they needed. There was a well chewed arm, laying in the dirt in front of the den. Cameras were set up and soon they had recovered the arm and bagged it. It appeared to have been surgically removed. What was left of it, anyway.

So much for only a bag of old clothes and a car seat. Maybe that was all the Guard had found and decided it was what the hunters had seen, also. They might look into the Guard a little bit, though.

Chapter 6

He was so angry when he got home that he decided to go fix up some things in the shed before going in the house. He wasn't ready to bring his pet out to the shed yet and if he went in now, he might damage her too much to recover from and she would have to stay in the shed, then be discarded.

When he went in the house a while later, she could tell he was angry, but she did not realize most of it was gone now. She stayed super meek and quiet all evening and he absently patted her head before putting her in the kennel. Handling his trophies and reliving the best parts always put him in a better mood. Tonight, it didn't work as well as it usually did.

When nothing happened the next day at work or the next and nothing was on the news, he started to relax a bit.

***

"Have any of you heard anything about the body we found?" Jerry asked his buddies as they sat around in his living room a couple of weeks later.

"No."

"Nope."

"Not a word."

"Seems odd, to me. I would think there would be an outcry to find out who it was and what happened?"

"Another odd thing, when my apartment building caught fire a few days ago, I almost didn't make it out. I swear someone hit me as I came out the door to get out, but the smoke was so thick and so much stuff was falling, the Fire Marshall said it was probably just part of the building that hit me. I still thought I saw someone and he said something, then hit me." Said Pudge.

"They said it is definitely arson. All the exits were blocked, too. Just seems odd. The custodian has always been so careful about keeping those clear. It is a real shame he didn't make it though. It looks like part of the building frame hit his head and he was unconscious when that part caved in."

They were a somber group as they sat around. Usually the jokes were flying, this evening, nothing seemed all that funny. At least two people were dead and as far as they were concerned, neither were natural deaths. The body in the bag certainly wasn't. But why had nothing been in the news about it?

When the phone rang, none of them were surprised to find it was the Troopers. The Officer they had talked to in town wanted to see them. He wanted to know when he could speak to all 4 of them and Jerry told him all four were at his house, currently. He asked if he could come over and if so, would be there in less than a half hour.

There was a fresh pot of coffee on and cups out when the Officer knocked on the door. After seating themselves around the table, the Officer asked if he could record the conversation so he would have it correctly, any time he needed to check anything said. They agreed and he turned on the recorder. Everyone's name and identity was stated for the record and they started talking.

He asked them to retell finding the body, what it looked like, describe the photos they had taken and what they had done following discovery.

After he shut off the recorder and they had all relaxed a bit, he asked if they had any questions. Of course they did and he would not be able to answer most of them on an ongoing case, but he made the offer, anyway.

"Why haven't we seen anything about it on the News?"

"Someone moved the body between you seeing it and us getting there. We did find evidence, but we don't want the person that moved the body to know that, yet. Maybe, if he thinks he got away with it, he will get sloppy or put it back. That is about all I can tell you for now and I would appreciate you not asking around about it, too, please."

He turned and looked at the bandaged up Pudge and asked what happened to him?

"The apartment building I live in burned a couple of nights ago. Jerry has been letting me stay here until I find another place and can fend for myself a bit better. By the way, he has become a fairly decent cook. Can you believe it?" Pudge answered.

"Didn't at least one person die in that fire?"

"Yes, the custodian and now they are trying to blame him for all the exits being blocked, but he was always careful to make sure they were open. He took pride in his job."

"Do you think it could be related to what we found?" Pudge asked.

"There is really no way of knowing, but be careful and pay attention to everyone around you. Without evidence, who knows?"

After the Trooper left, they continued talking about the body and the fire. At least now they knew why no mention was made in the news. It made sense, which helped, also.

***

When he came home the next night, he was furious. The damn girl pulled a knife on him. Damn near got him, too. He pulled his shirt aside to check the slash along his ribs. Just a little bit one way or the other and she might have done it. He grudgingly smiled. She'll never do that again and should have learned how to use the tools she carried. Now he had them.

When he walked in the house, Éclair's eyes got huge and round. He must have looked a sight. "It's my blood," he growled. He went to the sink and dampened a towel to wash some of it off and see exactly how he could patch himself up. When he turned, he was surprised to see the girl looking at him and making motions asking if she could help. Humph, if she didn't handle anything sharp, maybe she could, at that. He handed her the towel and she gently bathed the blood away from the wound. She could tell it was only a surface cut but had bled a lot. She motioned for the antiseptic and held it to him, so he could do it himself. She really did not want to cause him any pain at the present. If she ever got the chance, she would not only cause him pain, she would rid the world of him, but that time was not now.

He gruffly told her to go ahead, he knew it would hurt and he would not punish her for it. She delicately dabbed it on as he sucked in his breath. Then she blew on it to lessen the pain. After it was dry, she held out her hand for the butterfly bandages he had on the table and he handed them to her. She was doing it a whole lot better than he could have managed on his own.

Once the butterfly bandages were in place, she covered the area with gauze and then fastened it in place with pieces of tape. It looked very professional. Maybe she was a nurse. Didn't matter, time to eat then she would go in the kennel. He was going to be sore tomorrow and not able to show it. At least his job didn't require heavy lifting.

***

Jerry filed his paperwork to run for office. It was early and he would have quite a while to line up everything he wanted to do, if he got elected. His District was a small one with mostly folks like him in it, so he thought he could represent them pretty well. He went through the State budget line by line, questioning every single expenditure and found ways to cut the budget in huge amounts. If the State could not maintain what it already had, why should

41

they be considering enlarging the need? It didn't make sense to him, so he printed out copies of what he proposed and handed them to his buddies to comment on. He figured they would give him honest answers.

"The villages will love you and Anchorage and probably most of Fairbanks, will hate you. Don't give up your day job." Marky offered as his advice.

"Well, maybe half of Fairbanks will actually go for this, if you present it right." Pudge chimed in.

"Aw, if you present it right, you can probably get well over half the State to back you on it. I would suggest starting small, say on social media and post suggestions for ways to do all of these things, yet do them cheaper or with less Government involvement in them." Put in George.

"Yeah, people get fired up on there and pass the posts around and before you know it, you will be elected before the election," Marky said.

"Maybe this will be the first election in Alaska to be run on-line."

They wrote out several short potent posts to start placing and thought they had started the ball rolling now. By next election, Jerry Cameron should be a household name.

George, being a computer geek, set up a web page and a public social page geared towards Jerry being elected and started publicizing them both.

***

He was looking for a place to rent or buy somewhere farther out of town. Somehow, he would find a place more suited to his living style. He would really like to find property that was off the grid, if possible, although with his job, that might not be possible. They liked their people to be on call.

Removing the trash bag with the last plaything in it and replacing it with the bag of old clothes and other bulky items was inspired. Now anyone finding anything would not know exactly what had been there. Finding another place was not difficult here, there were huge areas with no access or people around. Look how many had never been found over the years.

He walked in the door and found the girl in the bathroom instead of on her bench, where she was supposed to be. He casually punched her in the side of the head, knocking her off the seat. She didn't move from where she landed, half under the sink and he walked back into the other room, leaving her lay there.

After a while, she crawled back out and pulled herself up onto the bench and sat there. Her face looked lopsided and he thought maybe he had broken her cheekbone. She had to learn.

When he put her in the kennel that night, he rubbed his hand down her injured cheek and watched the tears run down her face. But she did not make a sound. When she moaned in her sleep that night, he kicked the cage and she went quiet.

After he left the next day, she looked in the bathroom mirror and tried to push the bones back in place a bit but lost consciousness and had to leave them the way they were. She had to find some way out of here, wherever here was. She was determined to survive and if possible, kill the man.

She started looking at everything as a possible weapon. The two rooms of the house that she was confined to, offered nothing to work with and she only walked in front of him, to and from the bedroom. She would have to check the kennel over better.

This room was impossible to pick anything apart in, with the spycam on her all the time. The bathroom didn't seem to have anything in it, either. She grabbed her stomach and went into the bathroom as though she had to use it. She knew he checked and would question whether she was in there too long at a time.

She found that the curtain rod was a round rod slid into another round rod and appeared to be much too long. She bent a piece over at as much of an angle as she could manage and worked it back and forth until she broke the end off. Then worked the rod back together and put the curtain back up.

Now she had a short piece of round curtain rod. She needed to sharpen the end. First, she needed to find a place to keep her weapon until it was ready to use. She still would not be able to stay in here very long at a time nor too often during each day.

Chapter 7

When Jerry checked his website, he was surprised
to see a few hits on it already. The comments were
positive, then he realized they were all from George,
Marky and Pudge. But still, it was a pleasant start to
his day. He decided to use his bike as it was
probably one of the last nice days before winter set
in. He was usually very much a man of habit, so this
was an unexpected last minute change to his routine.
When he got about a mile down the road, he heard
an explosion behind him and turned back toward his
house. His nice pickup was scattered in burning
pieces all over his yard.

He called it in, not as a 911 call as it was not an
immediate danger to anyone. If he had used it
today, he would not have even known what hit him.
The entire drivers' side of the pickup was missing,
seat and all.

While he sat there waiting for the police and fire
department to show up, he tried to figure out what
happened. This was not some random act and since
he had just filed to run for office, it should not have
irritated anyone to this degree yet.

This suddenly made him feel like he was very
exposed, sitting out here in his yard on his bike.
Who hated him enough for this? He hadn't dated

seriously in quite a while and didn't think any of his past girlfriends was this mad at him. Most remained friends, he thought.

When the Troopers showed up, one had been involved with the search out the highway for the missing body. "Hey, you must have really ticked someone off to make them torch your pickup, Jerry. Or is this related to our last meeting, humh?"

"I really don't know, but why would anyone do this to me, regarding the missing body? I don't know anything."

"Well, it looks like it must have been on a timer, not someone watching and setting it off after you got in it, or you would not be here, right now. That looks like a lot of explosive was used so they really meant business."

"You mean someone has been watching me and knows my usual routine well enough they thought they would get me this way?"

"Afraid so. It sure looks like it, anyway. I will check the area a bit and see if I find where anyone has been watching from."

"You don't suppose the fire that took out the apartments where Pudge was living and this bomb have any connection, do you?"

"We'll have to wait and see. I would suggest you be very careful, your friends, too." The Trooper told him as he turned away to start his search.

***

He wasn't sure whether to give in to the anger he felt that his perfectly nice bomb had failed, or feel gleeful that that smug S.O.B. had something to

47

worry about now. The apartment building fire was fun, but somehow he had not hit the man there correctly or hard enough to keep him down in the burning building and the fire almost got them both. All his careful planning was not working out like it was supposed to.

He needed to sit down and write it all out. Then he could see where things were going wrong. He did his best planning when he could plan it as though it were for someone else. If he had followed his plans, last time, he would have escaped easily. That elderly couple he was watching back then had enough supplies and extra tanks on their pickup, he could have driven clear through Canada before he had to fuel up.

He had enjoyed sitting up on the hill above them, watching the old man work on the ancient dozer. Watching them through the scope of his rifle, he felt so powerful, knowing he could just pull the trigger and take care of one of his problems. When he returned to the dilapidated cabin he was staying in and wrote it all down on the stack of paper plates, he told the whole story. How he could do it and when he would make it happen.

There wasn't enough food in the old cabin, so he hiked all the side roads, finding cabins and trailers that all had some food stored in them. Maybe the man would have noticed that he broke locks on the doors. Anyway, he knew he would have succeeded if he would only have stuck to his plan.

If the road grader operator had not picked that day to come work on the side roads and check some of the places before the owners showed up, he would have been long gone. He panicked and shot at the grader, then ran. That was his big mistake. He varied from his plan. If he had just stayed still in the cabin, the man would not even have known he was there. So now, he needed to make another plan.

On his way home tonight, he would stop and pick up some legal tablets and pencils. Then he could make better plans, be professional about it.

The girl was sitting on her bench when he came in, her head was down, but she was sitting there carefully. When he raised her head up, her face was swollen and badly bruised on one side. He pressed into the bruised flesh and she cringed but did not make a sound. Tears leaked from under her closed lids, still no sound.

He smiled and went back into the kitchen to prepare something for dinner. She was learning quite well.

He left later that evening, going hunting, he said. He spent the evening driving around near the older bars and motels in town. Sooner or later, he would find the one he was looking for. Young, alone and maybe drunk, too much to understand what was happening until it was too late. He smiled again, thinking about how they usually reacted, once they knew.

Most cried, then begged not to be hurt. They were predictable. The girl was an exception. She had been hitchhiking from her broken down car when he stopped and picked her up. He wasn't even hunting that night. She was just a perfect opportunity. She did not drink, and when he turned the wrong way at the crossroads is when she asked to be let out. Then she tried to open her door and jump, but found the door would not open from the inside. Then she tried to roll down her window and it would not work, either, although she managed to get it partway down and tried to climb through it.

He grabbed her legs as she went out and hauled her back through. She was kicking and screaming the whole way and if any vehicles had come by, he would have been caught, red handed, so to speak.

As he dragged her out his door, she continued to hit and kick and even tried to bite him. He was so excited he didn't wait until later, he tore her clothes off her and had her, right there, beside the road. It had been such a long time since he managed that, he felt quite encouraged by her resistance. However, he couldn't get her home like this, so he hit her until she was unconscious and loaded her back into the truck and looked around for all her pieces of clothing. It wouldn't do, to leave evidence just laying around.

When he drove by the next morning on his way to work, he double checked the area to make sure he found everything. That one was really something. He would take his time with her, she was worth the effort.

Things had gone better since he got her, maybe she was his good luck. He didn't find one this evening, though.

***

George never saw it coming. He was walking down the sidewalk, minding his own business and then he was flying through the air, hit by a speeding vehicle. Witnesses said an older pickup, speeding way above the speed limit, just went right up on the sidewalk and hit George and right back onto the road without even slowing down and kept right on going. No one got a plate number or even a good description of the vehicle or driver. As hard as George was hit, there should be quite a bit of front end damage to the pickup, though.

George was on life support at the hospital, no one knew if he would survive or not. He had massive injuries, so even if he did survive, they did not know if he could ever function again. His pelvic bone and both legs were shattered and groin damage was severe.

Marky, Pudge and Jer stopped by every day to see him, and they talked to him as though he could hear them, which the doctor assured them that he could. They were trying to save his legs, as they were badly mangled. The other three men offered blood if it were needed.

As they talked it over, they felt like they were being targeted, but had no idea why. It's not like they were keeping some deep dark secret and getting rid of them would make sure it never surfaced again. They talked over the body they had found, trying to figure out if it was the pivotal point this all hung on.

They felt somehow that it was, but just could not make sense of why it was so. They studied the pictures they had taken, enlarged on a flat screen TV so that every detail stood out. They were missing something, but what?

They made copies of all the pictures, so each would have all of them on hand to study, although none of them really wanted to do so, by themselves. Somehow it seemed better, when they were together. As they were looking through the enlarged pictures, they noticed a shadow back under some trees on one side where there had not been a shadow in any of the other pictures. When they zoomed in on it, it looked like a person was crouched down, back there.

By now, Jerry felt like he had the Trooper they were dealing with, on speed dial. As soon as he answered and Jerry identified himself, he asked if they had noticed a possible person in the background of one of the pictures they had taken of the body, back in hunting season? The Trooper said no, they had not and which picture was it?

Jerry told him they were using a large flat screen TV and zooming in on the photos. They had not checked them all, but it appeared they may have been watched.

"Well, that would explain why you are being targeted now, if someone saw you there and has your information, somehow." The Trooper told them.

"Maybe they got the vehicle tag numbers and from the ATVs, also, to find out who we all are." Jerry answered.

"That would be one answer," said the Trooper.

"Do you have any other suggestions or reason to think that is not how he got our information?" Jerry asked.

"Oh, no, I was just thinking out loud and I don't have any theories at all about it. Thanks for calling me about the shadow on the picture and we will be checking them out a lot better, now."

After talking to the Trooper, the three men sat quietly, watching the slide show of pictures cross the screen. It was not something that they wanted to watch and finally, Pudge could stand no more and shut it off.

"Why don't we run into town and see George? I know he can't really join the conversation, but he does need us now."

"Well, I don't have a vehicle at present, so if we are going, I have to ride with one of you." Jerry said.

"We can all go in my car. It has plenty of room." Marky put in. "Maybe we can check it over before we get in it."

As a joke, it fell very flat.

Chapter 8

Tonight he was feeling great. He had beat her and she fought back, never making a sound, until he hit her damaged cheek, then she had moaned and passed out. He performed magnificently and felt on top of the world. He certainly showed her who was Boss.

He was hunting again, knowing he would find the one he was looking for one of these nights. As long as he had the girl, he didn't feel the need to rush into taking someone that did not meet all his criteria. She didn't fit his usual profile and he was not sure why that seemed so perfect for her. She was one of a kind.

He was cruising the streets near the older part of town when he saw the three men drive by in a large fancy car. Everything about them rubbed him the wrong way. They were fairly young, didn't have any money worries that he could see. Their looks were varied, from average to very good looking and they always seemed to draw the ladies when they were out in public. They were able to afford fancy cars and expensive toys.

He snickered to think how the one looked, flying through the air after he hit him the other evening. That one didn't look so great now, did he?

By the time he was done, none of them would look good. He needed to find more dynamite. Just his luck the one decided to ride his bike the day he had the pickup all fixed up special for him. Now that would have been something to see.

He followed them at a distance to see what they were up to and saw them pull into the hospital parking lot. .Ah, they were here to see their buddy. How touching.

Maybe he should leave them a little something. He stopped and checked the contents of the bag behind his seat. Yes, that would be perfect.

The weather was staying pretty cold, but it was still starting to smell pretty bad. It had been a very pretty head a few weeks ago, but now it wasn't so nice. He could always get another one.

He parked at the edge of the parking lot and walked toward the hospital entrance, making sure to pass directly by the car they left parked close to the doors. As he approached, he pretended to be searching for his keys and checked the doors. They were not locked, so he quickly opened one and tossed the bag inside, onto the seat. Then he took off the surgical gloves he was wearing to burn when he got home. He had plenty more in his pickup, and wore them all the time he was not working.

He was so busy congratulating himself on what he just did, that he almost missed seeing the girl walking along the highway in time to slow down behind and observe her a bit. She walked unsteadily along, carrying on an argument with herself as she walked. He checked his mirrors and did not see any lights either direction, so pulled up next to her and lowered the passenger side window.

"Are you okay, Miss? Need a ride on this cold night?"

"No, thank you. I am doing fine." Then she stumbled into the side of his pickup. "Oopsie, didn't see that there."

Perfect. He was out of his truck and around on her before she completely recovered. He opened the door and tossed her up inside before she even had a chance to complain.

He popped her on the chin just hard enough to stun her and hurried around to his side and got in. As he was pulling away, he saw a light over off the side of the road, but it should not be a problem. It was too dark for anyone to see what just happened and he had no interior lights in his vehicles.

She was still groggy when he pulled up by the little shack behind his house. It had heat in it, so she would not freeze and he could play a long time before she wore out.

He bundled her into the shed and closed the door behind him. He felt almost giddy with joy. He not only found a new toy, he also left a present for those fellows that were a leftover bother from the other one. It was a good night.

He tied her to the metal bed frame and taped her mouth and eyes. This one would not work loose, each hand and foot were tied to a separate part of the frame. She did not look as athletic as the other one, so she would not be doing any gymnastics to get herself free. He threw a blanket over her, no use letting her freeze before he had any fun.

When he went in the house, the girl was sitting on her bench. She was looking pretty bruised up, but she still kept quiet. He would let her heal up a bit, now that he had another plaything, for a while. He herded her into the bedroom and locked her in the kennel. He almost told her what he had been doing tonight, then decided not to. She probably would not see the humor in it all.

***

When Jerry, Pudge and Marky walked in George's room, they were surprised to see that he was awake. His eyes lit up when he saw them. He wasn't able to talk or move, but he was back and he was aware. They held a mini-celebration, right then and there. A nurse came in to tell them to keep it down, but she understood. They were all happy to see George awake. The nurse removed the tube in his throat and he was even able to croak out a hello to them.

He tired quickly and his eyelids drooped down, so they said their goodnights and welcome backs and headed out to the car.

When Marky opened his door, he saw a black trash bag on his front seat. The smell was starting to seep out and he jumped back. Pudge saw it next, then Jerry. Marky pulled out his phone and called the Troopers.

The doors were dusted, but they figured they would not find anything useful. Then they took a lot of pictures and finally, they removed the bag. No one was anxious to see what it was. Finally the bag was rolled down enough to see the contents. The mutilated head of a young woman looked back at them.

Several turned away, sick to their stomachs. One of the Troopers offered the men rides home as they wanted to check over the car in case the person responsible had lost hair, fiber or some other piece of evidence that would help catch him.

"Jerry, how many bedrooms are in this house, anyway? Four? Five? What say you rent us each a room until this is over? I would feel better if we were together. If he gets one, he gets us all, that way and none of us has to go through being left without our best friends."

Jerry looked at each of his friends. They both nodded agreement. "We'll have to ask George, but he will need some help when he first gets out, anyway."

"We can move to the basement bedrooms when George gets here, so he won't have to maneuver the stairs."

They planned out the way to set up the house to make it easier for someone that wasn't getting around very well. The house had bathrooms that could be considered wheelchair accessible, even, so they were set.

Then they checked the webpages they set up a while back. The first responses were encouraging, even the ones left by strangers. Maybe Jerry did have a chance of getting elected. They needed to work on his campaign more and get it taking off on its own.

When Jerry did get his first interview, it didn't go the way he wanted. Everyone was more interested in the head found in Marky's front seat and what did it mean?

He could honestly tell them he did not know how, why or what reason there was for anyone to do something like that. He would like to see the Troopers get the funding needed to improve their forensic lab. If he were elected, that would be one of his projects.

When they watched the interview that night, on TV, they teased him about finally getting a plug in for getting elected.

***

What? The playboy was running for election? Who did he think he was, a Kennedy? Ha, he would make sure that never happened. He would have to think this through and see what he could come up with. Maybe post some of his private collection pictures on the web page and see how people reacted to someone that had pictures like that. The thought tickled him so much, he actually laughed. He was going web surfing.

She didn't know what changed his mood from irritated while watching the news to laughing out loud, but usually he treated her better when he was in a good mood. She relaxed a bit and tried to think about getting away.

He found the web pages and tried to hack into them. It seemed someone had a better security system than the prison system did. He was not able to get into their system to change anything. All he could do was post to it, and he was not ready to do that, yet. Especially not from his home computer. Maybe he would go to the library on his next day off work.

When he left the house, after dinner, she relaxed a bit, again. She did not know what he was doing, but any time he was not in the house, was a better time for her. Once, she thought she heard a scream, but listened hard and never heard it again.

When he came back in later, he was smiling, so everything must be okay. He herded her to the kennel, locked her in and went to bed.

After he was asleep, she started bending on one of the heavy wires that made up the kennel. It was located on the bottom where he could not easily see it and she thought if she ever got it loose, it would be one more sharp item she might be able to use to escape, someday. Quite frankly, she was surprised to still be alive.

He checked the shed before leaving for work and found the girl there, bruised and sullen. She would not respond when he poked her, so he poked her harder with a sharper stick. She reacted and he smiled, then left her sitting in the bed, tied hand and foot and mouth taped shut. If he got started on her now, he would miss work. He needed the job to continue his hobby.

Driving his newer pickup on the slick roads almost made him late for work. Not being used to it but having to drive it as the older one needed some front end work, since George. He kept one of his legal pads under his work sheet at work so he could make plans on what he wanted to do next. When he wrote this way, he wrote about himself in the third person. It helped him see things more clearly. The psychiatrists at the Institute said it meant he was crazy, and he liked letting them think that. It always looked good in Court. He had managed to fool the system a lot when younger, that way.

He took great pleasure in messing with the system. He studied every nuance of the Laws and how different verdicts could be achieved by saying certain things in just such a way.

He almost stayed in the Lower 48 after getting out of prison because the Courts down there were more inclined to go along with the crazy plea. Later, he always got better and they let him out. However, it was much too crowded for him to play some of his games down there. If he let one of his toys loose to run and for him to shoot at her, someone would not only see it, but film and post on the internet. If anyone was going to do that, it would be him.

Maybe he would try that with the new one. It had been a while since he did any target practice and hunting season was over now, so there wouldn't be so many people out in the woods. He would even let her wear some shoes, so her feet wouldn't get hurt too soon. The cold wouldn't bother her for long.

Chapter 9

The day George was released, the men all wanted to make it special. Just knowing he was going to survive, was great news before, but now he was actually getting out.

As they drove to Jerry's house, they decided to go on up to the truck stop and get to-go boxes and a pie to take home. George said after all that hospital food, he was ready.

Jerry called in their order so it was ready when they got there and Pudge ran in to pick it up and pay for it. It was only a few minutes to get to Jerry's house, and then they all settled in to do some serious eating. George found that he needed a nap after the meal, so they escorted him to his new bedroom and helped him get settled in.

When George woke up, he asked if he could get set up to go on-line and check out how they were doing. He wanted to try a couple of things, too. When he went in to the web pages he found evidence of someone trying to hack into them. He called the others in and showed them what he meant and how he set the pages to reflect any attack on them. He actually wrote some of his programs, so he figured no one should be able to get around them.

Why would anyone want to hack into a politicians' page? It certainly would not be for the benefit of the politician that is for sure. The more he thought about it, the more he wanted to know just what was up, so he wrote in another segment of program to follow anyone home that tried hacking in. That should prove interesting, if they knew enough to know he caught them at it.

The four men brainstormed a bit and decided on some press releases to send out. They listed what Jerry was for and what he was against. It sounded so straightforward, everyone should realize he would be great in Office. They questioned him about his past, and dug into anything that could possibly be used against him.

How about his family, were any of them apt to be an embarrassment? No, he said, he was about as radical as anyone in his straight laced family had ever been. He wasn't politically correct in a lot of ways, but not offensively so. He decided early on that only telling the truth was a lot easier than trying to remember lies, so tried to always tell the truth, even when he did not look all that flattering in the light of some of it.

Marky traded in his car for a newer one. He just could not like using the other one after he got it back, even though it had been totally cleaned, inside and out. He still had nightmares about the head found in his car.

Pudge knew a reporter for the local newspaper so they wrote up a release to give him and would offer him an interview, if he wanted one. They would send releases to all the local radio and TV stations, not that any of them were broadcast locally any more, but they might make it into the news.

***

When he got home that night, he was still slightly smiling, thinking of the game he had devised for the girl in the shed. He thought it would be vastly entertaining and thought he would see about setting up a video camera with a remote start on it, so he could film the whole thing. He had a perfect setting in mind, wide open country and she could run to her hearts content.

He had the next two days off, so he would take her out tonight in his old pickup. No one would see it out where he was going. The roads were not maintained out there, but not enough snow on the ground yet to keep him from driving in there, anyway.

He packed his bag in the bedroom while the other girl sat on her bench in the main room. She was curious, but not curious enough to try seeing what he was doing and getting hit or worse.

He set a bag of sandwiches inside the door and a case of bottled water. He would lock his bedroom and the door into the kitchen. She would have food and water and he threw a quilt on the floor by her bench. She could make do.

She made sure not to let her face show any emotion at all as he prepared and placed the food and quilt in with her. She figured he was going to be gone a bit and was just glad he was going to leave her alone and still alive. She wished he would let her wear clothes.

He looked at her long and hard, before he finished his tasks and she was afraid for a few minutes that he was going to change his mind. She tried her best to become invisible, but it never worked.

She knew the spycam was still on her so she could not even celebrate in a small way that showed, but inside, she was dancing around the room and whooping it up. She heard him stop the truck over by the shed and tried to see through the shuttered window without it showing on the cam, but could not really see between the cracks. Again, she thought she heard part of a scream, but the sound was choked off as suddenly as it started. Maybe a raven. There were a lot of them that stayed around. She heard them every day.

Once she was sure the truck was entirely gone, not just parked somewhere else on the place, she relaxed a bit and checked the bag of food left by the door. There were some sandwiches and energy bars, with some fruit in the bottom of the bag. At least she would not starve, depending on how long he was gone.

He stayed on the expressway and got through town without anyone seeing him in the early evening. The girl was under the blanket in the little jump seat, bound hand and foot and taped mouth and eyes. He headed south towards the closed for the winter Denali highway. It was quite a bit out of the way, but he thought he could have uninterrupted time there.

He heard the girl coming around about halfway to where he wanted to spend the night. She would not be comfortable, but too bad.

He pulled off the highway through a small snow berm and drove on in to the campground that was far enough from the highway to not be seen. It was a couple of miles back and the area around it was a nice open bowl of pristine snow. He grew excited just thinking how it would be, in the morning. He yanked her out of the backseat and threw her on the snow, pushing her back down as she tried to rise. Then he was on her and smacking her face back and forth with his hands as he forced her to submit.

After he was done, he pushed her back into the truck and slammed the door shut. He got back in the front seat and settled in to sleep a bit before daylight. Then the games would begin.

When he awoke, he could hear her sniffling in the backseat. He reached over the seat and casually cuffed her, snapping her head against the door. She was no sport. He hoped she did better, once she thought she was going to get away.

He set up his camera and set it for wide angle to get the best possible shots, no matter which way she ran. Then he pulled her out of the truck and yanked the tape off her face. She howled in pain and he slapped her. He undid the rope around her wrists and ankles and she tried to kick him. Good, maybe she did have some fight in her.

He stood up and pointed to the horizon, visible to the north as being the closest way out of his sight. She looked at him in disbelief and he looked at his watch, pointed to a 5 minute head start and pointed again to the horizon. She started to shake her head as he reached into the truck and pulled out a couple of rifles. Her eyes went wide and she took off running as fast as she could. Instead of heading directly toward the horizon, she started back along the roadway they had drove in, the night before.

He chuckled to himself and drew a bead on her, then he pulled away and fired a shot into the snow at her feet as she ran. She almost fell but caught her balance and renewed her efforts to make it out of sight. Next he grazed her side. She shrieked but kept running. Then he grazed her other side. She quit making any noise, saving her breath to run.

He pulled out another rifle and fired several rounds missing her but herding her a bit so she stayed in the camera view. Then he nicked her arm. First at the wrist, then the elbow, then closer to the shoulder.

By this time, she was bleeding quite freely, but he was still just nicking her, here and there. The blood spattering on the snow made him feel like an artist, so he tried for different patterns from different placed shots. Then he shot through her shoulder on the right side and then the left. By now, she was stumbling around, not managing to run, at all.

When he got to her, she was still breathing, but not running, still, she did not collapse. She looked at him and spit in his face. He knocked her down and had her again, right there on the film he was shooting, which he didn't even remember. Then he started dismembering her. By the time she gurgled her last, he was well into removing arms and legs. Then her head. He smiled as he remembered what he had done with the last one. Maybe he could do a repeat on this one. Make it part of a political statement for the one running for Office. Wouldn't that make a good plank in his platform?

Chapter 10

Jerry was feeling optimistic about his campaign. So far, it appeared to be the right message at the right time. Everyone was fed up with the status quo in Juneau. Yes, he knew that most people started out on a smaller scale, testing the waters by filing for local elections first, then working their way up to State level and then on to the Federal stage. He had no desire to attempt to make any changes in Washington D.C. and the local politics would not affect what he was passionate about. So he had decided to go after what he wanted to work with and see how it worked out.

The worst would be that he lost with only 3 or 4 votes of his friends and himself. The best would be if he won by a landslide of popular acclaim. Somewhere in the middle would be fine by him. He knew he would not be popular with the ones in power now. He just hoped enough people were fed up enough to vote for him even though he was not running on any of the established platforms. It was a fine dream, but not very realistic as a lot of people were fond of pointing out to him. "You have a great platform, Jerry. But you don't have a snowball's chance of actually winning so a vote for you is just wasted."

Why couldn't they see that if they all actually did vote for him, well, he might just win? Radical thought, but it would work.

George was testing out using a walker now instead of the wheelchair he hated. He was slow but determined and it gave him plenty of exercise, cussing it out as he slowly worked his way down the hall. He found Jerry in the dining room, where the formal table that was never used anyway, was inundated with piles of paper and reports. Somehow, there was even a full copy of the State budget with all of its special interests well represented. He finally managed to get himself sat down in a chair at the table and reached for the pile of papers closest to him.

"Do you want me to go through the budget with you and we can make notes on what is necessary and what is pie in the sky?"

"Sure, another set of eyes reading this over might make some sense of it. Tell me again why the Governor gave the oil companies huge tax breaks after they have been enjoying record profits for the last few years? I really cannot see where that helped the State of Alaska in any way and certainly isn't helping the people of the State."

"Looks like we will be about two billion dollars over budget this year and it gets worse, as it goes along. They are just looking for excuses to tap into the Permanent Fund and no funding for pensions is just the perfect excuse. However, if they peeled some off the other special interest items, there would be funding. Let's put some of this as the first steps on the ladder to getting the State back on its feet."

"Hmmm, sounds like some sort of slogan there, George. Maybe write that down somewhere, so we can mess around with it. We need something to get people's attention." Jerry said.

When Pudge and Marky got back from work, later that day, they talked about what George and Jerry had spent the day working on. They were all ready to dive into the budget and see where things could be taken out or changed around a bit to actually balance the budget if not have a surplus. It had been done in the past, it should be possible to do it again.

When there are X number of dollars coming in, then don't spend more than that amount and if possible, even less. Housewives all over the world learn to live within their means, why can't Government?

The charts they were making showing where the dollars were going looked depressing. Maybe they could use them in ads to get people to start thinking. Voter apathy was the largest block to their campaign.

***

When he returned home, he parked the old pickup out back, out of sight from the main road. Then he loaded up his camera and sleeping bag and brought them into the house. When he checked the spycam, he saw the girl, seated on her bench. Her head drooped as though she were tired and feeling magnanimous, he decided to let her go to the kennel early this evening. When he unlocked the door into the living room, she jerked upright but kept her head down a bit. She picked up the folded quilt as she headed for the bedroom and he unlocked the door, letting her in. Then he locked her in the kennel and left the room. He wanted to check out the video on his large screen TV.

He left the doors open between the rooms and she could hear the sound, although it was muffled some and she did not know if it was an actual TV program or movie. She hoped it was a movie. The sounds of the girl sobbing and begging made her choke up and she buried her head under the quilt, trying to drown out the sounds.

It sounded a bit too much like her situation for her to ignore it and when the shots started and the screams, she almost lost it. She still did not make any sound, but the tears would not stop. Her fingers found the piece of wire she was working on, so she used this time with the noise in the other room covering the noise, to work faster on breaking the wire loose.

When it came loose, she almost fell over. She was not expecting it at that moment. The piece of heavy wire was almost a foot long, so she bent it over for a handle and started trying to figure out how to make it even sharper. She knew if she ever had a chance at all, it would only be a brief chance and she had to make it count. She thought if she ever had any opportunity, it probably would be in the other room, so had to find a way to hide this wire in there, without it being found.

She found a similar piece of wire on the other side in the bottom of the kennel, and started working on bending it, since she had one out. The more she could have around the place, the better her chances of getting to use one someday. She almost missed the TV being turned off. She immediately settled in and covered herself with the quilt. Maybe he would leave her alone if he thought she was asleep.

For several days, he put her in the kennel early and watched his video. He never tired of seeing it over and over again. Even when he starred in it, no one could have identified him. He always had the knit facemask over his face and most of his winter gear on. Even when he jumped her, not many identifying features showed. Maybe he would use this one on the Politicians' webpage.

Then a helicopter had spotted the bloody snow while flying security over the pipeline when they wandered a bit off their usual path and someone took pictures and leaked them to the TV station in town. They were on the air before the Troopers even knew what was happening. They had recovered tissue samples and some fibers and hair at the scene, but no body.

No, they would not find the body unless he decided they would, he thought. Maybe the head in the guy's car would be funny, again. He now had a nice new car. Guess he didn't appreciate the little gift left in his other car. Well, too bad for him.

He hiked in from the back of the man's property, to leave his little "gift" in one of the vehicles again, if one was unlocked. Sure enough, the first one he tried was not locked. He set the head in the front seat, so it was looking right at the door for whomever opened the door. This should be funny, he thought, as he eased the door closed and walked back the way he arrived.

***

Pudge and Marky left for work and since they worked not far from each other, they took turns driving and sharing the expenses. It saved on finding parking, also.

Jerry was working from home and George was not driving yet, so the tampered with car was not noticed until almost two weeks later.

Jerry was going to start the vehicle up and move it, as it was just sitting there in the way at present. The ravens squawking around it every morning wasn't exactly like a rooster crowing to wake a person up. It was fairly annoying and right beside his bedroom. When he opened the door and saw what was on the seat, he threw up. Then he went in and called the police.

By then, any external evidence was long gone and the snow was trampled so much, no one could tell where the grisly gift had come from or who had left it. The Troopers came and did a complete search and took the vehicle to the shop to thaw and vacuum out for any possible evidence. They didn't think they would find much.

"Man, I hate this. Why is this jerk targeting us? It's not like we know who he is and could I.D. him or anything." Marky said.

"At least he didn't get one of the vehicles we actually use a lot. We would not have noticed that until spring if the ravens hadn't of been arguing around the doors." Pudge mentioned.

"Still, we better start keeping everything locked up. Who knows what the man might do next. Or what if it is a woman doing all of this? We just assume it is a man." George reminded them.

"Is that being politically correct or what, George?" they teased.

"Well, you just never know. It could be some really twisted, ticked off lady." George countered.

"Safe to say, if so, she ain't no lady." Pudge answered.

"Yeah, that's a given."

"I still think it is a man." Jerry pitched in. "That shadow on the photo looked pretty good sized for a woman. It just didn't look right to be one."

"I don't think it IS a woman, I just mentioned it might be, as we are all assuming it is a man. I hate to just make assumptions." George said.

"You are right, George. We have just been assuming and that may lead to mistakes. We should make some charts of when and where we have been targeted, even the apartment fire might not have been an accident. We will put everything on it and see how it looks all together."

"Just don't mix it in with the political stuff. I don't think this would be so good for the campaign, Jer."

***

He was disappointed that it took so long to find the head in the car, but he happened to be nearby when it was found and laughed when the fool got sick when he opened the door. What a bunch of

78

sissies. He probably could just forget about them and leave them alone, but they were fun to play around with. He had not been able to hack into their web pages. Whoever set those up really knew what he was doing. He would have to see if he could find a way around and still get in. Maybe post some video or still shots. That would really "help" the man's campaign.

The girl was looking like she was losing more weight and he finally realized he was not feeding her again. He seemed to be getting a little bit forgetful lately. Going to have to watch that.

He started leaving a dozen boiled eggs where she could peel and eat one whenever she wanted, besides heating up a frozen meal every evening for her. He bought doughnuts every time he thought about it, so she now had some on hand all the time. Soft drinks weren't healthy, so he bought cases of juice in small containers for her. He didn't want to be accused of starving his pet to death. He was still trying to figure out just why he was still keeping her as a pet.

He had not felt the urge to go hunting lately. The last one was almost more trouble than she was worth. He did still enjoy watching his video and sometimes playing some of his older videos from a few months ago. The last one was his favorite. Everything showed up in detail. The camera was so much better and caught all the sounds, too.

It was a surprise that the site had been found so soon. He didn't know the helicopter crew sometimes flew quite a distance away from the actual pipeline corridor. He would have to remember that for the future. Either find a copy of their flight schedule or make sure he would not be in the vicinity during one of their flights.

Maybe he was just feeling like hibernating a while, just like an old bear. He had fancied himself a trapper for a while. He even talked that Judge into helping him get guns and ammunition for his new career. The Judge was an interesting man, he only saw the good in people though, so he always had to watch for and not show what he was really thinking or planning on doing. Too bad the Judge got caught.

Chapter 11

Jerry was scheduled to give a speech and found he had stage fright. He knew the subject and knew he was well practiced in it. But here he stood, behind the curtains, sweating and feeling faint. Even worse, he knew most of the people that would be the audience tonight. Friends, family and coworkers, mostly, with a few reporters and a camera in the back and one over to the side of the stage. That was it, the cameras. He never liked having pictures taken as he was not really photogenic, he thought.

Then there was no more time and he was out on the stage and being greeted by the MC for the evening, Pudge.

Pudge soon had him at ease and the rest of the evening went very well indeed, he thought later as he really didn't remember much of it. Pudge told him he opened his mouth and gave his speech with some very good ad libs thrown in and was a hit, but he could not really remember anything beyond the deer in the headlights feeling he had when he looked directly into the main camera.

When they got a copy of the speech to go over later, he was amazed. He looked like he was having a good time and really did do a good job on the speech. Wow. Maybe he could do this.

His main platform for his campaign was simple, "Get some common sense into Government" and someone pointed out that it should now be considered uncommon sense as it seemed sadly lacking in any form of government.

George set up a bank account and all the necessary paperwork for accepting contributions and just seemed to be a natural as campaign manager. Being on crutches or if he would be required to stand very long, confined to the hated wheelchair seemed to put his brain into high gear and he was really getting a kick out of running the campaign.

Pudge and Marky helped when they could, but they both had regular jobs to continue working at. They did keep Jerry and George up to date on what was being talked about, around town.

***

The girl knew he was furious when he slammed the outer door on his way into the house and cringed inside. She did not have any way of staying hidden and she was afraid he would take out his anger on her, yet again.

When the locked door swung open, she was sitting on her bench, trying to look serene. He stopped just inside the door and looked at her. He wanted to just walk over and slap her, but she was looking so ladylike just sitting there, he just couldn't go ahead and do it. She always had a delicate air about her that looked fragile, yet he knew she could put up a fairly good fight, regardless of her small size.

He almost wanted to teach her some self-defense moves. Now wouldn't that be weird? Kidnapper teaching the kidnapped how to defend herself. He almost smiled at the thought and his anger seemed to have disappeared. Without saying a word, the girl somehow managed to calm him down. She was worth keeping around just for that. His temper was usually what got him caught, in times past.

He walked back in the kitchen and brought in two frozen meals and offered her the choice of which one she would get that evening. She looked surprised yet pleased, so he felt good about letting her choose. Of course if she got to be a nuisance, she was outa here, just like the rest.

After dinner, he decided to go check out the house where the four men were living. They were getting complacent as he had not bothered them in quite a while. Of course, they really were not doing anything to him, so he probably should just forget about them. Something bothered him about them though. They seemed to have everything they wanted and no real problems in the world. Why should they get everything in life just the way they wanted it? All he ever wanted was to just be left alone to enjoy himself and there was always some smug person butting in on his fun. Well, he could mess up these four smug people and enjoy himself while he was doing it.

When he climbed the small hill behind the house, he had quite a bit of snow to wade through now. He did not realize just how much had fell in the last couple of weeks. If he came back up here, he was going to have to wear snowshoes or just find a better place to keep them under observation. They did not draw the drapes across the large windows, only the smaller curtains in the bedrooms and kitchen. With his binoculars, he could see detail inside the house from his observation point.

When he scanned across the walls in the living room, he quickly swung back as something caught his eye. Why, they had two big charts on one wall, one with pictures where the one body was first deposited and the other was something to do with the campaign he was running. So they WERE trying to do something to him. He was right to be doing all he could to get them first. Wait a minute, they only had the things he had done to them on the chart, and maybe they had not made the connection yet. Hmmm, he would have to think this over.

When he returned to the house, he put her in her kennel and went to bed, himself. No matter what, he had to still go to work tomorrow. He would think on this some more.

When he left for work, he left early enough to swing by the house where the four men lived. Two of the vehicles were already gone and one was warming up. So that was why he had messed up with the second head. He did not do his research and picked the wrong car, although it still was rather funny when it was found. It was worth it for the entertainment he got from watching them react. They were such sheltered young men. When he thought back to things he had already seen by the time he was their age, he had to smile. They would probably faint or puke. That would be a hoot, to toughen them up. Men should not be such weaklings and the one wanting to be in Government? He needed to get some backbone and learn how to work other people to the best advantage. He actually seemed to think he could trust people at their word. What a fool.

When he got to work, he continued thinking about the four men and how he could jangle their nerves and toughen those boys up, make men out of them. Maybe make them another one of his projects, just not in the same manner as his usual ones. He had to laugh about that and a co-worker asked him what was so funny. He told the man he was just thinking about his pets.

His replacement didn't show, so he had to pull a double shift. He wasn't too upset. He had plans and this would give him more time to think about them and think them through so there wouldn't be any stupid mistakes, apt to get him in trouble.

On his way home, he spotted a drunk girl, weaving her way along the side of the road, carrying on an argument that she evidently had been having for a while. This was too good to pass up, so he slowed to a crawl behind her until there was room to pull over. Just as he approached her, a State Trooper vehicle pulled up beside him.

"What seems to be the problem?" the Trooper asked him.

He just about panicked, then realized the officer was not accusing him, he was asking.

"I was on my way home from work and saw this lady in a dangerous situation and was going to try to convince her to sit in my warm pickup while I called to see where she should be dropped off. I'm afraid she may already have some frostbite. Now that you are here, you can take over, Officer. I need to be getting home. My pet hasn't been fed or let out today and I had to work overtime." So saying, he walked back to his pickup and signaled, then pulled out onto the highway and headed on home.

The Trooper called in backup. He did not want to try manhandling a belligerent drunk into his car to have her claim brutality later, after he saved her life and got her warmed up again. His video camera was recording everything, so he would at least have evidence of her condition and actions.

When he approached her, she swung at him and fell on her face in the snow. She did not move. He returned to his car and took a heavy blanket out and covered her in it, until he had help picking her up. At this point, he called for an ambulance.

He was a little upset, not that the girl got away, but that he was positive the Trooper had the camera on and now had him on record as stopping to pick up a woman. He would have to be super careful for a while, now. Of course, he was still wearing his uniform and maybe that worked in his favor. No one would actually check and see just what type of uniform it was.

***

Jerry had another speech to give. He was trying to convince himself that he was going to do okay and would remember giving the speech this time and not faint or get sick to his stomach. George worked with him and knew he had it down to perfection, if he indeed did not faint or puke. "Jer, just what are you afraid of? You know the speech subject matter inside out and have it so memorized that you can say it in your sleep and just might have done so during the night last night. At least I think I heard you giving your speech in your sleep."

"You actually did hear me giving my speech last night but I was awake, just practicing. I don't know why I panic every time I just think of looking out at a sea of faces looking back at me and I just know I am going to flub it. I have to resist the urge to look and see if I have my pants on or if I remembered to zip them. I just don't know, but I feel so sick I really don't know why I ever thought I wanted to run for office. Tell me again, huh?"

"Jer, you know you can do this. You know what your subject is and you have a lot of really good answers for the questions everyone is asking. It would be for the good of the State if you win. So, get out there and do it, tell these people just why they should support you, tell their friends about you and what you plan on doing to earn their votes, now and in the future."

"Okay, I guess I am as ready as I will ever be. Ack, don't push me." And he practically fell out onto the stage to begin his speech.

Later, he lightly punched George in the arm.

"Gotta work on a better way for me to make an entrance. That was almost a disaster, tonight."

"Got you out there, didn't it?"

The next night he had another speech and turned to George as he clung to the curtain.

"So you are going to do that every time I stall on going out?"

"Yes, or something similar. You have to give these speeches if you want to get elected, so steel yourself to it."

"Is it going to sound like whining if I whine a bit?"

"Yes."

"Alright, guess I gotta suck it up. I am so afraid of messing this up."

"Just go with the tried and true little trick of looking at your audience and picturing them all naked." George told him.

While he was still laughing, George pushed him out onto the stage and he was on.

As usual, once he actually started giving his speech, he did fine. He was humorous yet got his point across about the need for some real changes in how Government worked. It was supposed to work FOR the people not beggar the people it is supposed to represent.

They had worked long and hard finding all the ways the budget could be changed to reflect actual need instead of the current spend until you drop method. Repairing roads, bridges and buildings, instead of building more and letting the ones already in place fall down around their ears. It was a good message and something that needed brought out to the public and made an issue. Even if he didn't get elected, maybe he could affect the way things were done in Juneau.

Chapter 12

He was sitting in the audience, listening to the man speak. He had thought to heckle the speaker, yet found that he was agreeing with a lot of the message. It was going to be harder to cause problems for them after listening and liking what he was hearing. He should have stayed home or gone hunting. When had he developed any sort of conscious? No, he still didn't have one, but he was older now and could see some things a little bit more clearly, maybe. Just like keeping a pet. He certainly never even considered doing anything like that before. It must be old age.

He kept his hat on and stayed quiet. When the speech was over, he left as soon as possible. No use having them recognize him, if they saw him again.

When he got home, he was tired, so put the girl in her kennel and went straight to bed. Somehow this evening did not turn out as he expected and planned for. Time to make more plans.

He woke up feeling grumpy and did not improve as he prepared for work. He cuffed the girl because she was too slow getting out of the kennel. Her nose started bleeding and she tried to hold it so it would not splatter on the floor. He booted her into the other room and she skidded across, smearing more blood.

He went into the kitchen and got some wet paper towels and tossed them to her, telling her to clean up the mess in his room first, she could work on this room after he left.

She scrubbed the floor as well as she could, holding a piece of paper towel against her nose to keep it from dripping more and finally got all she could see. She brought the used paper towels back into the living room and he had a sack ready for her to drop them into. He seemed almost phobic about keeping any blood out of the house.

He set a bucket of water and a roll of paper towels in the room by her bench and locked her in. The trash can was by her bench, also, to put the used towels into.

When she was done, she double checked to see if she had missed any, as he was apt to punish her if she left stains. Her eye was swollen and her nose didn't look any better, from being hit. But it wasn't as bad as it could get when he was angry. She was thankful for small favors, even when she still got hurt.

***

At work, several of the crew were talking about last night's speech and wanted to know if it was as good in person, when he said he was there. They had only read the newspaper and couldn't tell if the reporter was accurate or not. Since the news started to reflect the reporter nowadays instead of just reporting facts, no one was ever certain, any more.

He told them, that in his opinion, the man gave a good speech and his message was straightforward. He thought he just might even vote for the man. He certainly couldn't do more harm than the ones in office were already doing.

"Yeah, you got something there, Art. Maybe I will, too." One of his co-workers told him.

He had to laugh to himself. Who would ever have pictured him influencing someone on who to vote for? What a laugh.

***

Jerry felt pretty good about his speech last night. He didn't feel quite so ill while on stage and never once thought he was going to pass out. Progress, he thought. The reviews continued to be favorable. Then George told him he had to fly to Anchorage, he had an interview set up and a speech directly after at one of the hotels where a group was holding a meeting and looking for a candidate to endorse.

"Remember, look at them as if they were all naked and you are the only person in the room wearing clothes. Just don't let your imagination embarrass you if some of them are really good looking." George told him.

"Aren't you coming with me?"

"No, at present, we only have funds for one plane ticket and I don't want anyone saying we are using private funds or misusing donated funds." George explained.

"You are running on fiscal responsibility and that does not include someone coming along to hold your hand." George continued.

"Okay, I can see your point, I just hate flying and I don't know the town of Anchorage at all." Jerry responded.

"Well, Jer, that is why you call a cab at the airport."

"Gee, thanks. You sure know how to keep me from getting a swelled head over any of this."

George had his ticket and hotel reservation in a folder for him and Pudge offered to drive him to the airport. He was going to be cutting it fine to make it down and to the hotel on time. George figured this way, he wouldn't have time to get stage fright.

When he returned the next evening, very late, he was very tired. He thought the speech went well and the men that talked to him afterwards had a lot of ideas for his campaign.

However, he felt that they also had a lot of strings attached to him accepting their backing. When he told them that, they assured him they did not want to change anything he was saying or wanting to do. Somehow, he wasn't convinced and did not give them a solid yes or no. He would think it over and see what the future looked like.

He did not want to just join the current holders of office and do the same things they were doing. That would negate his reasons for running in the first place.

George, Pudge and Marky agreed with him. He certainly didn't want to accept endorsement nor backing that would be counter to his entire campaign. Getting compromised this early would just be a painful reminder that he was a novice and inexperienced. He wrote the offer on the large poster they had on the wall for the campaign. Just one more line on a mostly blank page.

It was reason for them to feel pretty good about the whole idea of Jerry getting elected. If someone took him seriously enough to make this offer, they must think he had a chance of getting elected. By the time they settled in for the night, they were very optimistic about the upcoming election, next fall.

When a Reporter called and asked to set up an appointment with Jerry for an interview for statewide viewing, they knew he was being taken seriously by everyone. George set up the time and place with the Reporter and they would meet in town. George wanted to keep Jerry's private life just that, private and if they let a Reporter do an interview on TV in his home, it would be up for public comment and debate. He didn't want any outside factors to intrude on the message Jerry wanted to give.

After the interview was over, the Reporter sat and talked to Jerry and George a while. He was a seasoned older gentleman and had much experience in the political scene of Alaska. He told them he was giving some free advice and it was worth every penny. But not to trust anyone in the business and no one that seemed out to help without looking into their background very carefully.

He told them the story about a first time Legislator that went to Juneau and wanted to help, but accepted an invitation to dinner with some seasoned politicians and lobbyists at a famous downtown hotel. The man was flattered that he was being included and told everyone up front that he wanted to make his first vote the next day, count.

The man didn't make it to the vote the next day or for many days after as he was confined to his room with a horrible case of not being able to leave the bathroom. His dinner had been liberally laced with laxatives. They do not play fair in Juneau and it wouldn't hurt to be a lone wolf until he got the hang of it.

They thanked him for his advice and for doing the interview. Jerry felt he had been fairly portrayed. Even after they watched and recorded the interview, they still felt good about it. The man was a true professional and did his job very well. George figured he actually liked Jerry or would not have shared that story with him.

Now that he was getting popular for speeches and interviews, Jerry was finally starting to relax a little bit and seldom had the urge to puke or pass out before or during a speech or interview. The cameras were kind to him and he looked good on screen.

He was even pleased with the editing done on his first big interview. He sounded very intelligent and not as fumbling as he thought he did. No one had cut and snipped his words to make him sound like a halfwit and that was always nice.

Some of the others were not so kind, but no one did a hatchet job on him yet. Maybe the first one set the tone for the other reporters. They didn't want to look bad in comparison to the fine Reporter that did the first one. He could only hope that continued.

***

When he got to work, the first person that saw him asked if he was going to the debate scheduled this weekend for the people running for office. It was being held in Fairbanks, which was unusual. He had not even thought about it as he usually didn't pay any attention to politics or politicians. He probably would not have, this year either, except he was watching one of the men running for office.

What the heck? He might as well go. He didn't have any game tied up at home at the moment. He snickered to himself over that one.

When he got home that night, he checked on line and found tickets to the debate and bought one. He checked some of the sites he followed and went to the webpage set up for the man running for office.

Whoever was maintaining it was very good at his job. He could not hack into it and the page looked very professional.

The girl's face was healed up, again. Her eye just had a bit of yellow and green bruising showing yet around under it. She shivered a lot, as he never kept the house very warm. He knew when he was gone, she kept the blanket wrapped around herself. He did not allow that, when he was home. Maybe he should let her have some clothes. No, she was a pet.

If a man was going to have a pet, it should be a well behaved pet and she was. He could not complain about her manners. She did not even show an attitude with him which he knew she probably wanted to do, but was afraid of the consequences. Very smart, on her part.

He had not found another girl yet, that fit his preferences, so he was starting to get antsy. He was going out more often in the evenings, looking. It had been a while since he hunted so long without finding one. Either word was getting around, even though he had not read or heard anything about it, that girls were going missing or the cold weather was keeping them in. He thought most of the current crop of girls were not as tough as they used to be. The cold weather never stopped him from finding girls before.

He enjoyed the debate far more than he thought he would. His guy made excellent points and was hard for the others to refute what he said. His guy? When had that pain in the butt become his guy? Oh well, he had a vested interest in the man, he figured, so he was glad to see the man made a good opponent.

On his way home, he was not even hunting, when he saw a girl weaving her way down the side of the road, stumble into a snow bank and just lay there. He slowed his pickup and parked so his lights illuminated the fallen girl. If anyone stopped by, he was just checking someone in trouble.

When he got to her, she was unconscious. He picked her up and put her in the back seat of his pickup. If she regained consciousness and was combative, he didn't want to wreck his truck trying to stay on the road and fend her off.

When he got home, she was still out, so he pulled around to his shed. He had not seen another vehicle since he picked her up. He draped her over his shoulder and unlocked the shed door, went in and closed it behind him before turning on a light. Wow, he must be living right to have one just fall at his feet, so to speak.

He stripped her and tied her hands and feet to the bedframe, then debated taping her mouth. If she got sick, she could choke herself if she was taped. The shed was fairly sound proofed, but a scream could be heard a long ways. He tied a cloth around her mouth that she could throw up around and might muffle any screaming she might choose to do before he came back out.

This one was a gift, so he would have to plan something really special for her. He covered her with a couple of quilts and turned the heat up a few degrees in the shed, so she wouldn't freeze if she kicked the covers off. Even with her feet tied, she might manage that, so he wasn't taking chances.

When he went in the house, he was feeling so content that he gave Éclair an extra treat. He kept a box of candy in the kitchen and seldom ever ate a piece himself, but the girl seemed to enjoy the chocolates. Tonight, he gave her two.

Chapter 13

Jerry was feeling so pleased after the evening's program that he invited his friends out to a nearby place for a late dinner. They spent the rest of the evening, savoring the food and good conversation as they dissected the entire debate. They would receive a copy of the video but for now, they just enjoyed thinking about it and considered it a win for Jerry.

By the time they got home, they were all more than ready to call it a night. Jerry was driving his new 4 wheel drive crewcab pickup and parked it near the house, hoping the security lights would alert him and scare off anyone planning to bomb it. He was still a little spooked to just get in and drive any vehicle. He always wanted to check under it and under the hood.

The next morning, he turned on the radio searching for news and went out for his newspaper. Yes! There it was, the headlines named him the winner in last night's debate. Now it wasn't just his friends saying it, it was official. Because the newspapers were always right, right?

They shared a laugh over that, over their morning coffee. After the paper was read, they tacked it to the poster board in the living room. The little news clippings were starting to add up. Now if he started showing well in the polls, they would relax just a tiny bit. None of it was set in stone until after the votes were counted and they still had a long ways to go. The Primary wasn't until August. Then if he won that, it was a major race to the November election.

Marky just hoped he wasn't doing so well too early and then people get tired of his speeches and lose interest. Since it seems that today's constituents have the attention span of a flea.

He told Marky not to disparage his future constituents, they were a very intelligent perceptive group and he was lucky to be running in such a good district. Marky told him to stuff it, he wasn't in front of an audience at the moment.

Winter was progressing quit well and they were starting to plan what they wanted to do before the end of winter. So far, they had not taken the time to go out snow machining in the White Mountains like they usually did each winter.

There was rumor of an ice bear roaming in the White Mountains this winter, tearing into cabins. So they decided that would be their excuse for taking a trip out to see if they could get him. The winter ice bears are usually an old bear that did not put on enough fat during the summer to survive hibernation, so they stayed awake, searching for more food, all winter. If they started hibernation in poor condition, they usually did not awaken in the spring.

Sometimes it was because they had an abscessed tooth and couldn't eat very well of just worn down teeth that interfered with their eating. Either way, they would not be in a good mood and not something anyone wanted to have breaking into a cabin they were trying to sleep in.

The bears usually developed a layer of ice in their fur, making it difficult to hunt them. Unless hit just so, a small caliber bullet didn't have enough power after penetrating inches of ice and before guns, the Native people sometimes tried spearing one that was causing problems.

They would use as long a spear pole as possible and antagonize the bear into attacking. Then they would brace the base of the pole against the ground and hold the shaft, hoping the bear would impale himself on it in a fatal area. The man holding the pole usually got injured at least a little bit and the ones antagonizing the bear into charging had to be very nimble to escape injury also.

George teased them about only using spears to make this an authentic ice bear hunt, as when he was a kid, it was still an accepted method of hunting grizzly bears in the State of Alaska. Now the Hunting Guidelines did not list hand held spear as an approved method of taking.

Since he was now getting around using a cane, the other men wanted him to try coming with them, as a hunt without him would seem wrong. He said he would pass on this hunt, he wasn't fond of going out looking for something that was apt to also be hunting him. He preferred to be on top of the food chain for his prey, not part of it.

He did feel left behind when they pulled out of the driveway and he was waving from the house. He thought he might just stay in all weekend and play video games or start a new ad to run for the campaign. As he thought about it, he thought maybe a new design would help keep the message fresh and keep people talking about Jerry which if it was positive talk, should help, in the long run.

When Jerry reached the parking area they planned on using, there were no other vehicles parked there. Word had gotten around about the bear and no one wanted to actually find him. They were starting to wonder if this was one of their less brilliant moves, also.

However, they were here, so they unloaded and fired up, ready to go. After a few hours riding, they did find possible tracks, but they were very old and partly filled with snow. The belly drag groove was all that told them this was not a moose wandering through. They glassed the entire area and did not see any recent sign, so decided to stop near here for the night and camp. It would be dark soon and they did not want to run into the bear after dark.

While they were setting up camp, Pudge kept looking around. After a while, he asked the other two if they felt like they were being watched. Jerry said he felt uncomfortable, but wasn't sure why and Marky hadn't noticed. They strung wire around the camp and hooked up the 12 volt battery pack to it. Usually that deterred most wild animals from intruding into camp. Pudge said he would feel better it is were 120 volt and barbed wire. Marky told him now that he mentioned it, he would really like that, too.

They let the fire die down and then went to their tents. They would be warm enough as they had very good gear, but none of them were very relaxed, so it was a few hours before they finally all dozed off to sleep.

The moon rose almost full and lit the entire mountain top in pale light. The aurora was faded out by the moon, but still added some glow and color to the scene. When the disturbance came, it really didn't surprise any of them when they thought about it later. But at the time, they all panicked. The roar that sounded through the stunted trees was bad enough, but the fact that it was still headed their direction made it worse. If sound was any indicator, the electric fence had royally ticked off the intruder. He was not happy and he knew who to blame.

Every small tree in his path was shredded before he continued on, which gave the men time to get untangled from their sleeping bags and out of their tents. The moonlight was bright enough that they did not need artificial light to see the bear when it stood up on its hind feet just inside the clearing they were camped in.

Jerry was prepared and had his rifle aimed when the bear stood, he fired. He kept firing until the bear no longer moved. While the adrenalin was still pumping through their systems, they loaded the whole bear on the sled behind Jerry's machine. No one wanted to try skinning it out in the dark, even if it was very bright from the moon. Jerry tore out the date on his harvest ticket and they went back to bed. Somehow, they even managed to get some sleep.

They were up and breaking camp as it started getting daylight the next morning. They were on the trail back to the trailhead before the sun came up and just as the sun was finally making an appearance, they arrived at the trailhead and started loading their machines on the trailer.

George was surprised to see them pulling in the driveway before dark. He half expected them to stay out as late as possible. He was even more surprised to see the bear on the trailer.

When Jerry backed the sled off the trailer and pulled it over to his heated garage, they opened the door and he pulled the whole works right inside. It would be simpler to thaw out in there and then they could skin it out. It would have been impossible at the camp with all the ice in the fur.

When everyone returned home the next evening, George had the bear almost completely skinned out. "Hey, just because I didn't get to go on the trip, don't mean I can't still help out on it. This is my contribution to the bear hunt."

"Thanks, George, I really wasn't looking forward to having to skin it, tonight, after working all day. I know my job isn't all that demanding, but still, I did work all day." Marky said.

Pudge offered to skin out the paws as he was a good skinner and took the time needed to do it right. Jerry would skin the head out. He was meticulous about doing a careful job on it. He took the time to split the lips, ears and eyelids, so when he was done, it was ready to take to the tanner. Of course, first he would have to have it measured and sealed at the

Fish & Game office. He cleaned the skull as much as he could, without boiling it, then salted everything so they could roll the hide up and bag it for sealing, tomorrow morning and the skull, salted and placed in another plastic bag to take along to seal and have a tooth pulled to age the bear. He loaded the bear hide and skull into the back of his pickup so it was ready for tomorrow. Then the men all went in the house.

When Jerry stopped at the Fish & Game office the next morning, George was with him. Jerry backed the pickup to the garage doors where bears were taken in for sealing then they walked up front to find someone to take care of it. Neither saw the man slip onto the loading dock behind them and add a little extra to the bag with the head in it.

When they walked back with the man from F&G and opened the overhead door to unload the bags, the F&G man carried the bag with the skull in it. As he placed it on the counter, he said, "I thought you only brought me one skull to seal."

"What? We did. Don't open that yet and call the Troopers, please."

The Trooper they had been dealing with was in and came right over. "What's the problem, boys?"

"I'm not sure, but there may be more than just the bear skull in that bag. Joe said something about thinking we only brought one skull in and so I think there may have been something added. Whether in my driveway after we went in last night, although the security light didn't go on, or here on the loading dock, I don't know."

"Oh, we have a security camera on the loading dock. If there is anything in that bag except what you expected, we can see if it was added, here." Joe said.

The Trooper pulled on surgical gloves and opened the bag. There, in the bag, was a bear skull and the head of a young woman. Her long hair spilled out over the bear skull, her eyes wide with horror. Joe had been peering over the Troopers shoulder and turned to puke in the sink. "I'll be right back and we can watch the video."

When the video was set up, they saw the edge of a pickup stopped just beyond the corner of the building and a man dressed in heavy winter gear approach the loading dock. He carried something in his left hand and reached into the back of the truck to open the smaller of the plastic bags and dumped whatever was in his bag into the other one. He turned and walked away, back to the truck and backed out so they could not even tell what color the truck was.

"Well, we know about the size of the person, but that could have been anyone, dressed that way. None of us could positively ID the person on that video." The Trooper said.

"I knew it had been too long since we got anything from that person. I still can't say if it is male or female, but I sure wish we could stop them." George said.

"Yes, this is four young women that we know for sure that have been murdered. I think we are going to have to alert the public that there is possibly a serial killer in the area. So far, we have been trying to keep it low profile, hoping the person would get sloppy and we could catch them."

"I've been wondering why we never see anything in the paper about any of this. I worry about the people I see hitch hiking along the roads." Jerry said.

"I just wish Jerry wasn't around when these show up, it isn't the best thing to associate with his campaign." George said.

"If it would help catch this person, I would willingly give up the political campaign. There is nothing more important than stopping this person." Jerry replied.

"I agree, Jerry, it's just that he has taken part of my life too. I wanted to have a family and a wife, not in that order, but now that is improbable. Yet I get to wake up every morning, knowing that will never happen. These poor young girls will never have a life or family and their families are left to wonder just what happened and why her?" George answered.

"Let's go home. Well, after they seal the bear and I drop off the hide at the tannery. This is kind of depressing."

Once they returned home, they looked at the charts they had started. Now there was a new addition to make on the first chart. One more girl to add. So far, they had no names to place with each addition. It was a very depressing chart.

***

He was having a very good day. He had not had
the time to play much with the new one, but the
results were worth it. He truly wished he could have
been in the room and seen the expressions on their
faces when they realized what was in the bag. He
was tempted at the time to park out front and just
walk back to see.

His good mood lasted through the evening until he
caught the 10 o'clock news. There he was, walking
up to the pickup, leaning over the side and dumping
the surprise into the other bag. What? He had not
even noticed the security camera mounted near the
overhead doors. He was slipping and some little
thing like that could be the end of his fun and
games.

At least he was well covered in winter gear and no
one could tell what he looked like or if he was even a
man. Ha, next time he would wear a long wig and
let some of the hair show. That should perk them
up. A good thing he parked far enough back or they
would have his license number and make of truck.
As it was, they only had a piece of one corner of his
bumper. It was a homemade bumper, so not even
that was going to tell them much. There were
dozens just like it in the area.

From the earlier euphoria he was now feeling
subdued and a little bit worried. What if there was
another camera there, where he didn't see it that had
his pickup on it? He was going to have to perk up
and pay better attention. He really didn't want to go
back "inside". Almost 20 years was enough.

The girl didn't know what had changed his mood, but she tried to stay as small and quiet as possible. She didn't know how much longer she could last, as he tended to get more violent with her now than he had for a long time. She was also worried that her mental strength was ebbing. She certainly didn't want to end up one of those girls that felt sorry for their captor. What she really wanted to do was kill him. That feeling worried her a little bit too, but not that much anymore. All she needed was opportunity, she would handle the rest as it happened.

When he put her in her kennel, she double checked her sharp hooked wires. She now had 4. She also had the piece or curtain rod in the bathroom. She just did not know how or when she would get to use any of them. She just prayed it would be soon.

Chapter 14

Pudge found the next "gift". Someone had attached a girl's hands to the bear's body where the feet had been cut off when skinning. The hands were loosely sewn on.

Pudge came screaming out of the garage like a little girl, Marky told him.

"Yeah, I learned it from you when you found that head in your front seat." Pudge told him.

The Trooper was pretty sure the hands went with the head found with the bear skull. He hated to think there was yet another girl dead. He was going through all the missing persons files whenever he had some time and there were several unaccounted for.

"You might want to keep all doors locked around here." The Trooper told the men.

"I am positive I did lock it when I came in. I seldom leave any door unlocked." Jerry answered.

"So we add lock picking to this person's many talents. Too bad he doesn't seem to have a conscience. He could do very well in the legitimate world."

"Somehow, I don't have much pity for him. His victims never have a choice or chance. Too bad he doesn't pick one that has a gun on her and knows how to use it." Pudge said.

Pudge almost got his wish.

***

He saw the girl walking along the road. She wasn't staggering as though she had too much to drink. She was weaving a bit, as though she was either very tired or very cold. He followed behind her a little ways and she never turned around, just kept plodding on. He pulled up beside her and reached across to open the door. "Get in the truck."

She ignored him and kept on walking. "I said, get in the truck." he shouted at her.

She slowed but still kept walking. "No, thanks. I'm not hitch hiking," she said over her shoulder as she plodded on.

"Get in here or I will shoot you." He yelled at her.

She looked directly at him, pulled up her right hand and fired the revolver she carried under her bulky jacket. The bullet barely grazed his arm, but it shocked him that he was actually shot. She stood looking at him holding the gun ready to use again, depending on what he did next. This was a tired girl, but she certainly was not a drunk one.

He stomped on the gas which slammed the door and took off. He tried steering with his injured arm and applying pressure with his other hand over the small wound. His arm burned like the very devil and he was steadily cursing as he pulled into his driveway a while later.

She had seen him. Not very well as he had the interior lights off in his vehicles, but the dash lights still illuminated his face a bit. She might be able to identify him, if she ever saw him again. This was not good. He would have to be very careful for a while and see what came up on the news.

The girl knew something was wrong when he came into the house. She could hear him muttering and cursing and fumbling around with stuff in the kitchen, so she sat very still and tried not to flinch when he unlocked the door and came into the room with her.

She was surprised to see blood dripping off his fingers of the arm he held cradled to him while he cursed under his breath. Good, he was suffering a bit, too. She kept her face neutral so he would not know she was pleased to see him hurting. When she was sure she had it under control, she slowly raised her face to him.

She motioned to ask if he needed her to help him doctor his arm. He gruffly told her yes and brought in supplies. She gently washed out the wound and handed him the bottle of antiseptic. He grimly smiled as he poured some on. She blew on it to ease the sting and he held still while she bandaged him. It truly was a very small wound. Even if he had gone to the hospital, they would not have stitched it.

She hoped by patching him up each time he needed it, maybe he would treat her better or improve her living conditions. It didn't happen, but at least he didn't hit her or anything else, so she considered the evening a success. She had long ago lost track of how many days she had been here. It didn't seem to matter anymore. Somehow, this was now her life and she was surviving it the best she knew how. But just give her one good chance to change her circumstances and she would take it.

During the night, she heard him muttering and tossing in his sleep and hoped he was getting an infection and fever. Then felt ashamed of herself for wishing bad on anyone. Then carried her argument a bit farther and felt she was justified in hoping he became extremely ill. Maybe he would harm no one else while he was laid up.

He still went to work the following morning, but she knew he was not feeling well. He looked flushed and stumbled a few times while getting ready to leave. He tossed some food into her room and locked the door. She heard him pulling out a short time later.

She was positive he had not been gone long enough, when she heard a vehicle pull in. Then she hoped it was someone else and she could scream and they would rescue her. But if she screamed and it WAS him, he would make her pay for making noise. While she fretted in indecision, she heard the door unlock and knew for sure it was him.

He unlocked the bedroom door and went in, falling across the bed. Was this her chance? She edged toward the bedroom door to see what he was doing and thought he was unconscious. She slowly worked her way to the door to the kitchen. It was locked. Her shoulders slumped in dejection just as a heavy hand fell on her right shoulder.

"Ha, thought you could leave, did you?" he mumbled.

She shook her head no and motioned getting something for him to put on his head.

"Oh, you want to help me, do you? And I am supposed to think you are just going to fix me right up and not try to get away?"

She shrugged as though she didn't know and just stood there. She felt that the next few minutes might determine her immediate fate.

He seemed to be thinking it over, then pulled the key out of his pocket, unlocked the kitchen door and marched her on into the kitchen. "Get what you were looking for."

She found a plastic container and some zipper bags. She motioned for him to fill the container with snow from outside and she looked for some over the counter pain pills. He thought about it and went out after some snow. She filled one of the baggies and handed it to him to use as an ice pack over the swollen arm wound. He took the pain pills and told her to prepare soup for them both. He sat at the table, watching every move she made. When she had the soup heated and found some crackers and sat everything on the table, he told her to eat and he sipped at his.

After they were done, she offered to replace the dressings on his arm and he let her. The wound looked ugly and red around it. Signs of festering showed, also. She heated a large pan of water and had him soak his arm in it, with some antiseptic poured in for good measure. When the wound was clean looking again, she handed him the bottle to pour more on the wound. Then she loosely bandaged it, thinking fresh air might be better for it than covering it tightly.

She washed up all the dirty dishes while he was soaking in the hot water, then cleaned the kitchen. She always hated housework, but right now, it was the best thing she had been allowed to do in ages.

She was still hungry, so motioned an offer to make sandwiches for a snack. He was feeling better so told her to go ahead. She made them both large sandwiches and ate hers as if she had not ate in weeks. By the time she was done, she was finally feeling fairly full.

He was feeling sleepy, so told her to get in her kennel, he was taking a nap, so she went along docilely, hoping he was feeling more kindly toward her. She wasn't paying close enough attention and stumbled as she went through the doorway and he smacked her hard enough to make her ears ring. No, he wasn't going to change now, just because she was being helpful.

***

Jerry knew he had an actual chance to be elected when the anti-hunting group attacked him in the papers. They would not have bothered if he were too far down the list to be noticed. The fact that the ice bear was dangerous did not matter, they were against anyone hunting.

The anti-gun group joined in. He was sure he had offended others and would soon be hearing from them, also. He was not insensitive to actual suffering and inequalities, but the fancied and made up offences actually irritated him. He was walking a fine line between trying to appease someone and not being true to himself. He would not be elected by kowtowing to any special interest group, whether it was Idiots Without Boundaries or Occupy My Back Yard people.

People that wanted something for nothing and expected folks that actually did work to pay for their wants and gimmee's irritated the hell out of him. He did believe in helping folks that truly needed a hand and sometimes there was a fine line between ones that truly needed and ones that only wanted. The ones that truly needed usually were not demanding. They might not even ask. Most of them had something the others knew nothing about. They had pride and self-respect. They knew that respect is earned, not demanded.

He and George sat together designing a poster laying these thoughts out and the differences between them. He would lose some voters, maybe, but he hoped to gain the ones that counted and made the difference in how things were done.

Even if he never got elected, he wanted someone to start thinking and maybe that person could influence someone else until more people stopped and thought about the things happening in today's world.

He thought he had started that process during the debate. He had put out several ideas that he thought made sense and by the end of the debate, he knew several people were following his lead. He had heard more people talking about his ideas lately. THAT was why he was running.

George had set up another speech for him to reiterate his stand on many of the popular problems facing Alaska at present. His stance was not always the popular one, and he wanted people to know why he thought some things should be put off and others pushed forward right now.

He wanted answers to some questions, like why did the State put a question on the ballot for public input, when it had already allotted the funds in the budget and let the contract out for the construction, as was done on a section of highway that would go right through a corner of wetlands and be impossible to maintain without massive amounts of money being spent to repair the damage that would be done every year from natural freeze/thaw cycles.

The City of Fairbanks had done the same thing over the years, but this was a statewide blatant disregard of due process and a waste of money besides. The cost of adding the question on the ballot and tallying the vote, if nothing else.

Politics seemed to bring out the worst in people, once they got into office and he truly hoped he had enough strength of character to remain an honest person and true to his beliefs.

As he prepared for the curtain to rise, he heard noises over behind the podium but was used to the stagehands moving around back there. As the curtain went up, something came down behind him and only George had presence of mind enough to push him forward and drop the curtain again. Jerry stood in front of the curtain with the mike in his hand and went ahead with his speech.

He heard more noises behind him while he spoke, but no one paid attention and everyone listened as he continued. He answered questions from the Press after he was finished with his speech. As he walked off the stage front, he wondered about the sounds he was hearing behind the curtain, but knew George would tell him as soon as he saw him.

A Trooper motioned him to come back while the room cleared. He walked back and thought he was going to lose his dinner. The "thing" that descended as the curtain rose was a composite body made of several different bodies, it appeared, or one that had been dissected, then reattached. It was not a fresh body. The heavy curtain had filtered out the odor while he was speaking but now, it was overpowering.

Just why was this person stalking him and his friends? Was this the person's idea of a joke? What kind of monster did things like this?

These questions and more whirled through his mind.

Chapter 15

He was upset. Why did the crippled guy have to go and ruin his masterpiece? He should have made sure when he hit him, that he did a better job of it. Maybe even visited his room at the hospital and made sure. This would certainly have gotten everyone talking about the guy running for office and had he not heard that there was no such thing as bad publicity?

Here he made the effort to prepare this little surprise, even though he was still suffering from his injury. He still had some fever and the wound was still a bit infected, he thought. He felt very disappointed that he had not managed to see the entire scenario unfold as he planned it.

When he returned home, he was still in a bad mood and the girl tried to not be noticed. As usual, she failed. When he walked in the room, he swung and she ducked with the blow so it only grazed her a bit but she fell on over so he would think he hit her hard.

That seemed to satisfy him and he walked on through to his bedroom, coming out in a few minutes and relocking the door. She remained on the floor, watching him under lowered lids.

He barely glanced at her and left soon after, locking all the usual doors behind him.

He was hunting tonight and felt in a vicious mood. He knew it was dangerous for him to be out in this mood as he would not be as careful as he should be. He drove his usual circuit of the bars and cheap hotels. Sooner or later, someone would have an argument and someone else would be walking home or even just outside a while to cool off, literally and figuratively. It was at least -30 degrees F out and anyone not dressed properly would be fair game.

He spotted a woman walking along the sidewalk but going the wrong direction. Then he thought about it and knew exactly how he could do it. He drove towards her, finally dodging toward her at the last minute and opening his door. She didn't even see it coming as she had her head down and the ruff of her coat over most of her face.

He swerved back onto the street and jumped out, leaving his door open. He scooped her up, staggered a bit, tossed her into the back seat, then jumped in, slammed the door and took off. He made several sharp turns to see if anyone was following him, then headed for home.

He was taking a chance on her coming to before he reached home. She was not restrained at all and could become a problem if she regained her senses. He tried not to speed at all, then breathed a sigh of relief as he pulled into his own driveway. It had gone very well so far.

He parked by the shed and hurriedly unlocked the door, leaving it ajar. Then around to his truck to retrieve his latest prey. He took her inside, closing and locking doors behind him. When he undressed her, he found that she was older and heavier than his usual toys, but she was still going to be entertaining. He usually picked smaller women as they were easier to handle. He tied her to the bed and a rag across her mouth, covered her with some blankets, and turned up the heat a bit. Yes, she might be a fun change of pace.

The girl knew something had changed when he came in the house, pleasant, almost jovial. He patted her on the head as he walked by and didn't smack her even once. She was afraid something bad was happening, or he would not be in such a good mood after leaving here so angry several hours ago. She felt guilty being glad he was being nicer to her but that maybe it was because someone else was suffering.

***

George was pleased that they had diverted most of the press away from the grisly scene behind the curtain and kept them focused on the speech. He spoke to one of the more inquisitive Reporters that he thought they could trust not to make a sensational story about this. The lead Trooper agreed and they allowed the Reporter to come back behind the curtain after everyone else had left. He lost his dinner.

After he recovered somewhat, he sat down facing away from what was on the stage and spoke with George and Jerry. They told him he would have an exclusive on this, but that they would appreciate it if it didn't get sensationalized. They had no clue why these things were happening and the Troopers were only now releasing some of the information, hoping to find the perpetrator before any more girls were taken. They felt he would be fair and impartial in his stories and they would contact him if they had any information or he could call them at any time.

A call came in while they were all still standing around talking of a missing woman. The Reporter perked up his ears, but the Trooper moved out of range. He tried to question the officer but was told not enough information was available and there was no use speculating at this time. Everyone was rather subdued as they left for home that evening.

They updated the poster they had of the grisly gifts they were given. They still could not find the thread that added them to his game. Because by now, they felt he was using them in a game of his own devising. Somehow, it was all tied in with the hunting trip or rather, the find at the end of the hunting trip. But how had he known that they were even involved in it?

Their names were never in any reports by the police and nothing was in the paper yet about any of that particular find.

Marky wondered what happened to the report filed at the Pump Station. That one not only had their names, it included their addresses and phone numbers. Pudge figured the guard simply threw it away, since all he found was a bag of trash.

They resolved nothing and turned in for the night.

***

He went out fairly early the next morning. He had all weekend and he wanted to do some target shooting. He loaded his gear in the pickup and went to see how his target was faring. She was struggling against the restraints when he walked in and the blankets had fell off the bed. She tried to scream, but the rag across her mouth muffled the words, but not the intent.

Good, she was mad. As he reached to finish uncovering her, she tried to twist away and he casually slapped her. Each time she twisted away or screamed at him, he slapped her again. It was starting to excite him and he began slapping and hitting her just because he could.

Later, he felt energized by his performance and untied her from the bed. While she was still unconscious, he would retie her and load her into the truck. It wasn't even daylight yet and he had quite a ways to go, before he found the area he wanted to use this time.

When he started to pull off the main road, he noticed a lot of tracks in the area and started looking around. Damn, someone had built a home back in here. That certainly messed up his plans. Maybe if he drove back out and took the next road in.

When he tried the next road, it too had a home built near the road and no access to the wide open areas he wanted to go to, farther beyond. Well, that was the pits, he didn't want to return to the area he used last time, as they might be watching that, now.

He finally found a road that was not well maintained although it had been plowed before the last snow. It looked like it was seldom used even when it was open in the summer. Trees hung over it, so he was getting hit by loads of snow all along it as he drove in. Excellent.

When he got to the top, he saw the perfect area to set up his camera and start his game. He heard muttering in the back seat, so she was coming around quite well. This time, he made sure his face mask was firmly in place so no matter what ended up on the video, he would not be recognized.

He had some new loads for his rifles and he wanted to check them out, so he placed everything in order on the tailgate of the pickup. There, everything set, now to get the star of this show out and moving.

She refused to run. What an irritating woman she was turning out to be. He jabbed her with a sharp stick and she glared at him but refused to run. Then he stabbed her with the stick, leaving it protruding from her abdomen. The shock on her face excited him again and he started loosening his clothes, then, she took off.

He grabbed up one of his rifles and shot her, just enough to graze her, then changed to the next one and shot her again on the other side. Her shoulders were now running red with blood and she was screaming obscenities at him. When he turned to pick up another weapon, she headed for him, pulling the stick out of herself and tried her best to plunge it into his neck. She did manage to graze him and she hoped he caught the hepatitis she was suffering from. She knew she would not leave here alive, so she decided to inflict as much damage on him as possible. She continued stabbing at him, managing to nick him here and there. His winter clothing was in the way too often for her to manage really good strikes with her injured arms, but she did hurt him. He finally slugged her and then shot her as he looked into her yellowed eyes. He continued shooting until most of his anger was under control. This game was not a fun game anymore.

He dismembered her and stuffed everything into trash bags. He tried to remember how many shots he had fired and picked up all the brass. He was bleeding from all the small wounds she managed to give him and the amount of blood from the final phase was everywhere. He pulled off his badly damaged parka and put on the one in the back seat, hoping to cover most of his wounds. Women had certainly changed in the 20 years he spent locked up.

He never imagined one let alone two or three of them would actually fight back. Girls used to be told to just go along and usually nothing all that bad would happen to them. Submitting usually made their captor be gentler with them, they were told. Ha, not on his watch.

He stopped at various places along the road and tossed the contents of the bags here and there. Left out, the birds and animals would take care of the evidence. He learned the hard way about burying them, they seemed to always be found, then.

When he got home, he parked out by the shed and used the small bathroom in it to shower in. He stuffed his bloody coat and clothes in the wood stove and started a roaring fire with some diesel. Then he made sure the truck was clean. He locked his rifles in the locker he kept for them in the shed after cleaning them. Then he made some notes about the various loads and called it a day.

The small wound on his neck was getting a very red angry look to it and oozing in a disgusting manner. He bandaged it after cleaning it up. The others seemed to just require the shower to clean them and a small bandage over each took care of it.

He was starting to think his game wasn't worth the playing. He seemed to be getting hurt fairly often now and that was never supposed to happen. He did not like it at all. He was supposed to be invincible and they were supposed to submit to his will. It was HIS game, after all.

He was starting to get lax about checking the girl before he walked into the room she was in. She was always where she was supposed to be and he liked it that way. She had not realized it yet, so it didn't make any difference.

Chapter 16

Marky felt like he was being followed and he couldn't understand why anyone would bother. Then he felt foolish for even thinking anyone would possibly be following him. Yet every time he went anywhere, it seemed the same pickup was always around. Yes, Fairbanks is a fairly small town, but it is larger than that. It was only if he was out in the evenings or on weekends. He never managed to get a picture of it, but he was now actively trying.

***

He was having fun following the little guy around. He knew the man was nervous and he enjoyed just showing himself often enough that the man could not forget he was around. He must be getting old, this was almost as much fun as the girls.

He didn't do it every evening or even every weekend, just often enough that the little guy never knew whether or not he would be there. He never even looked at the man when he ended up driving on by, as though he just happened to be in the same area.

He would use his other vehicle and follow the other one once in a while, just to vary his game. So far, the other one had not even noticed, huh? Didn't he have any intuition about his own survival? He was actually doing him a favor by teaching him to pay attention to his surroundings. He bet the one he hit a few months ago was more observant now.

He kept some tomatoes until they were very soft and took them with him one evening while riding around, looking for a chance to test out his theory that the one fellow paid no attention to his surroundings. He was in luck as there was no other vehicles on the street as he slowly drove by the house the other man, the tall skinny one, was visiting. Pudge had a sappy grin on his face as he came out to start his car. As he reached for the door handle, splat. A large warm ripe juicy tomato hit him in the back of the head hard enough to smack his forehead into the door.

By the time he got his balance and turned around, he saw only taillights making the turn at the corner. Now just what was that about? Kids having some fun? He, personally, saw nothing funny about it. He swore he heard laughter just as the tomato hit him, though. Weird.

As Pudge drove toward home, headlights stayed right in his mirror, when he slowed enough to let them pass, they just stayed right behind him, slowing down, also. By the time he made the turn onto the road Jerry's house was located on, he was starting to feel some fear. He thought of stopping and confronting the person behind him, then thought better of it.

As Pudge pulled into Jerry's drive, he thought the taillights looked like the ones he saw after the tomato hit him. What the heck?

He was having so much fun tonight. It reminded him of when he was a teenager and they used to do things like this. Maybe he was starting his second childhood. He still thought it was funny and the look on the skinny guy's face was priceless. He bet the guy was practically peeing his pants by the time he got home.

When he pulled into his own driveway, he was still chuckling. There were so many ways to entertain himself. He wasn't even hunting when he went out now, he was just watching those guys and seeing how he could play with them a bit. Maybe they would toughen up a bit and be real men.

***

Pudge was still wearing the tomato juice and pulp, so the others knew something happened. Marky said it was just some kids having fun, but he looked a bit spooked. When he told about the vehicle following him home, he was getting a little upset. Too many things had happened these last few months to just brush it all off as unimportant. They added a little side note on the poster they were keeping about the girls. They added Pudge's feelings of being watched, also. So far, George and Jerry didn't think they had been targeted.

George did pay attention whenever he was out. He certainly did not want to repeat his experience with the hit and run accident that he thought was not an accident. Someone did it deliberately.

Jerry was seldom out alone very much. He either had George or all of them with him. Working from home a lot of the time didn't make him as vulnerable to being watched, although once in a while he got that feeling right here in his home. Since the snow got so much deeper, he didn't notice it any more.

Jerry knew they had to have someone watching them quite a bit as the gruesome gifts always were timed fairly well with his activities. He suspected game cameras and didn't know where to look.

Of course, now that he was running for office, his itinerary was public and everyone knew where and when he was going to be somewhere. Once in a while he wished he never filed to run, but he truly believed he could help and make a difference. If nothing else, it was a license to harass the others involved and running for office, also.

He laughed when he thought of that. That was what Vogler always used to say. He never wanted to be Governor, but he liked to debate the other candidates and he said filing to run was the cheapest license he could buy to harass and keep them straight.

In Jerry's opinion, Political Correctness was just a term used to describe whiney, over-sensitive self-centered people that needed everything sugar coated for them. He had zero tolerance for them and figured he would lose a certain percentage of the vote just because of his attitude. He wasn't going to start lying to get elected.

***

He slapped the girl as he walked by her, no reason at all, just that he felt he was getting too lenient on her and didn't want her to forget her place, which was staying alive at his whim. He felt better when he realized he managed to hit her ruined cheek. It was still healing up and now was back to square one for it. He even had to chuckle a bit. He wasn't going soft, he was just taking his time.

It had been quite a while since he did any hunting and he had finally healed up from his own wounds. He did not feel all that good, but he thought he could at least go out looking. Maybe he was coming down with the flu.

He figured if he was going to have the flu, he might as well spread it around. After all, he must have caught it from someone, anyway. He asked the girl, once she was seated back on her bench, if she was feeling ill. She shook her head no.

She was afraid to admit it to him if she was, but she actually was not feeling ill, just sick at heart for being where she was. She did not think that was an answer he was looking for, so kept it to herself. He really did look a little ill. She hoped it did not mean he would just kill her to not have the problem of feeding her, but other than that, she hoped he was extremely ill.

Over the next few days, she noticed he was scratching his skin a lot and looked like he was losing some weight. Aww, poor him. She just could not muster up any sympathy for him. When she saw him rubbing his stomach as though it hurt, she secretly smiled inside. She was getting so used to hiding her feelings, nothing showed on her face.

Several days later, he felt well enough to go on with his plan to resume hunting. He still didn't feel

100% better, but he did not miss a single day of work and was going to continue with his game.

He was getting a bit more careful and watched several potential playthings continue on their way. Once he came close but at the last moment, noticed that she had someone sitting off in the snow where she was standing near the road. She was weaving back and forth and he almost stopped before he saw the other person raise an arm in a gesture to the woman to help him up. That had him nervous enough for that evening that he just went on home.

It was bound to happen sooner or later though. One night on his way home from work, he found another stranded vehicle along the road and a bit farther, a woman walking, alone.

He pulled over and opened the window near her. "Need a ride?"

"No, I'm just walking along, counting my blessings and waiting for summer." She answered.

Oh good, one with sass.

"Hop in and I can give you a lift to town."

She stopped and looked at him through the open window.

"Actually, I prefer to keep walking. My boyfriend will be along shortly and he will be looking for me, since he will see my car back there. I do thank you for the offer, but I really don't need a ride." And she turned and continued walking.

He was working up some righteous indignation at being rebuffed for being a Good Samaritan, here. Who did she think she was to not accept a ride when it was offered?

"Hey, lady, I didn't have to stop and offer you a ride. I'm trying to do the right thing here. Just get in the truck and let me do a favor, huh?"

She kept right on walking, ignoring him. Just as he started to jump out of the truck and haul her into it, he spotted headlights coming up behind them.

He closed the window and drove away. As he watched in the rearview mirror, he saw the vehicle stop and the woman get in. Humph, must have been her boyfriend, she must have been telling him the truth.

He was losing his touch. He didn't feel very good, so maybe it was best to just go home.

***

George was feeling depressed. He still was working on physical therapy, but felt he was not making any progress. He knew intellectually that he had and was making very good progress, but in his heart, he was still thinking it was not enough and he was never going to manage much more than what he already was doing. He knew the groin injuries were permanent.

Jerry was doing his best not to get irritated at George, after all, he was the one suffering. The rest of them were getting the fallout from it though and it was edging the household into open cabin fever. So he decided they were going to load up George and their snow machines and have a small side trip up to the White Mountains. They would use the easiest trail and not go very far, but they all needed to get out of the house for a while and open air would do them all some good.

138

George started to complain and then just went with the flow. He would ride as passenger on Jerry's large two seater. As preparations continued that evening for an early start the next day, he even lost the attitude a bit and helped pack some extra gear.

When they left the following morning, he was even cheerful. They all needed the time out in the wilderness. They stopped for breakfast at the truck stop just up the highway a bit and had sandwiches packed there, to take with them. They had trail food in their packs, but nice fresh sandwiches would be a better treat.

***

He was driving slowly by their driveway when he saw them pulling out. What perfect timing. He knew where the game cameras were located and knew how to get into the garage without triggering either one or the security lights. He hurried home and soon returned carrying his trophy from that last game he had played quite a while back. Most of it was dumped over assorted lookout points along the roadway, but this piece was still frozen in his own garage.

As he slipped into the garage after skillfully picking the lock, he looked around for the best way to display this one. He spotted several likely places but none looked exactly right. There was a basketball hoop set up in the far end of the garage. Ha, perfect.

He dragged a ladder over under the hoop and using some twine he found in the garage, he fashioned a second net weaving it into the hair on the head to hold the face looking out at them through the basket weave. He placed strands around the nose and mouth and each eye. He wondered if they would notice it right off or not even go into the garage for several days.

He decided to leave it open so they would know someone had been here. Not entirely, or the birds might fly in and mess up his display. He was chuckling to himself as he slid around the edge of the garage, still being careful to avoid the cameras. They probably did not still work at the winter temperatures, but why take chances? He made sure his face was covered at all times by a ski mask and he wore gloves to make sure no fingerprints would be found, either.

When he drove by a few minutes later, the garage door was only up a few inches, but noticeable. Yes, they would find his display. The overhead light he had dismantled and the work light aimed directly on it, would assure that. All in all, he was pleased with today's work.

Chapter 17

The four men had a wonderful day and George was back in form, laughing and joking with them. They even stopped and had dinner at the truck stop on their way home. They lingered over dinner. Such a perfect day was hard to bring to an end and somehow, going home meant the end to the day.

They agreed they would have to do this more often before breakup started. Winter in Alaska was just too good to waste.

When they pulled into their yard, there was already a State Trooper vehicle parked in near the house. Now what?

As they pulled in and parked, the Trooper got out of his vehicle and walked over to them.

"I have some bad news for you. I was driving by on my way back from a call and noticed your garage door open a bit. It was not open when I went out, earlier. Your Stalker has been by again and left a present in the garage. I don't think you want to see it, but so far, we have not touched anything. I want you to look around and see if anything has been moved or disturbed besides the obvious."

Jerry opened the garage door and noticed right away the interior light was not working, then he looked where the spot was pointing and almost lost his recent dinner.

"Why is he doing this to me? I don't even know who he is or where he is located. I think if I did, I would be tempted to go looking for him." Jerry gritted out.

"If we could figure that out, we would be out looking for him, also." The Trooper replied. "Well, actually, we are looking for him already, but we have no clues about who he is or where to start looking. It's best if you leave the man hunting up to the troopers, anyway."

"I know, but it is very disconcerting to keep finding these reminders that there is a monster loose in our area and he has no care for other human beings. It makes me sick to think what these poor women have gone through and then he leaves parts of them around as though this were a game."

"I think, to him, it really is a game. That is just my own personal opinion, though," the Trooper responded.

"Yes, I can see how it looks that way and he is thumbing his nose at everyone, proving just how smart he is and we are all a bunch of dummies." Jerry answered. "Of course, it is his game and his rules, so how he expects anyone else to know his game is beyond me."

"I would say he is not really expecting anyone to catch on to it, he just enjoys feeling superior because he knows his game and no one else does. He has an extreme case of entitlement mentality, to my way of thinking. He wants to do this, he is owed and he is going to do it, no matter who gets hurt. He probably does not even think of the ladies as actual people." the Trooper said.

"That is so sad for them. I just hate knowing he is still out there, still causing pain. Has there ever been anything like this around here before? I don't recall anyone ever being brought in on anything like this." Jerry asked.

"Hmmm, I think I need to go check back in the archives for information before I try answering that question and I better get back to work. I really should not be discussing an ongoing case with anyone, anyway. But you are involved in this and as far as I can tell, through no fault of your own. Just be careful and stay vigilant." the Trooper walked away.

By the time the crime lab folks were done and ready to leave, Jerry, George, Pudge and Marky wanted to go hunting again, just as they had with the bear. If only they had any clues.

***

He couldn't believe it! That blasted snoopy cop found it before the guys did. Just because the garage door was open a little ways, he just had to stop and look. He might just have to get rid of that cop. A nice explosion if he could find some explosives or a warming fire. Yes! A nice fire. He would have to follow and see where he lived. If he had a wife, it would be even better.

With his mind racing with ideas for getting the Trooper out of his way, he happily followed the man on his way back to the main office. Then he waited until the end of the shift and followed him home. He didn't follow closely and almost lost him a time or two as some areas had very little traffic. But he had stalked long and often and knew when to pull back and when to drive right on by.

He was disappointed not to see lights on in the house. Probably no wife. That could have added some fun to his getting rid of the policeman. He wasn't going to get fancy with this, just a simple gasoline fire should take care of the problem and he would be sure to block the exits as much as possible before setting the fire.

He stopped at a transfer station for trash and picked up several containers and old clothes. Then he stopped at a self-serve gas station and filled them. He figured the man should be asleep by the time he returned to the house and there were no lights showing.

He carefully positioned containers beneath each exit window and the largest around the doors. Once he had everything in place, he quickly went around the house, lighting the fuses made from old clothes stuck into each container. This would give him a few minutes at most to get clear of the area.

All were burning freely as he started up his pickup and drove away. He only made a couple of blocks before he heard the fire sirens. What? How could they respond so fast? Then he saw the volunteer station, just on the corner of the next block. The truck was already swinging out into the road and he pulled over to give it room.

Well, this one may not have succeeded. He took a chance and turned around, following the truck back to the house he had just left. The flames were shooting high and he did not see how anyone could have gotten out of it, alive. He parked across the road, out of the way and observed the firefighters hosing down the house and surrounding area. The ambulance was parked next to the truck, but away from the heat a bit, so he slowly made his way over to it.

There were a lot of other on-lookers appearing out of nowhere, it seemed. He got close enough to the ambulance to hear the EMTs talking and learned that the occupant was still in the building. Yes! Maybe he finally had one irritant taken care of. A fireman staggered out of the building, carrying a blanket covered body over his shoulder. When he was far enough away from the flames, they both dropped to the ground and the EMTs rushed over to care for them.

They pulled the mask off the firefighter and pressed an oxygen mask to his face. They uncovered the face of the man in the heat shielding blanket and started oxygen to him, also.

The firefighter sat up and held the mask to his face, removing it to cough a bit once in a while. "He was on the floor near the garage door. He had a pile of wet towels and blankets over himself, to keep the fire off him as long as possible. There appeared to be something barring the door from outside, so he could not get it open. He did everything right, so there is a possibility of him making it."

About that time, the figure on the ground started coughing, deep racking coughs. He tried to speak and the EMT leaned down close to him after he found he couldn't calm him until he listened.

"Anyone got a camera? Take pictures of anyone here watching the blaze. Do it now."

The EMT raced to the front of the ambulance and found his phone and started snapping pictures of everyone standing around, watching the fire. Some looked appalled at the damage, others eyes gleamed with avid pleasure as though they were at a fireworks display and it was set up for their enjoyment. He focused mostly on those.

When he returned to the patient on the ground, he could assure him that he took pictures, several of them as a matter of fact, of everyone around the fire. The man looked relieved and relaxed more, allowing them to work on him to bring any burns under control and get pure oxygen into his lungs. Then they placed him on a gurney and loaded him into the ambulance.

***

He was excited when he left the scene and started home. The man was alive, but they were guarded about his condition. Just getting him out of his hair for a few days was better than nothing and maybe the man would be a bit more careful now. Life was harsh, and he had to be on the lookout for his own survival. He felt like a teacher, trying to teach wayward students life lessons. The policeman, the four men, they all needed to learn.

The girl was afraid she was starting to fall into the Stockholm Syndrome and identify with her captor. She certainly hoped not. But once in a while, she felt sympathy for him and then it made her mad inside. She clung to the anger. She felt if she was to possibly survive the entire experience, it would be because of her anger. So she nursed it along and made sure any time she started to empathize with him, that she mentally slapped herself and went back to her anger. She would not be one of the idiots that begged for mercy for him.

She was slowly scooting her bench closer to the door he always came in through. She couldn't actually push it where she wanted as he still checked her video once in a while, so she would sit on it as hard as she could, letting it slide a fraction of an inch at a time. Not every day, but once in a while. Somehow it seemed important to be in defiance, even if it were only this small deed.

He smelled of gasoline and smoke when he came in. He locked the door to the kitchen and went straight in and showered. When he came back out, he looked very pleased with himself. She worried any time he looked like that. She didn't know for sure just what he did, but she figured it could not be anything good.

He unlocked the kitchen door and brought in a bucket of fried chicken and several side dishes. He looked around, then decided they would eat in the kitchen at the table. She was startled by this change in routine and not sure if it were a good sign or a bad one, but went along since there was no alternative. He even placed the food in the microwave and heated it all up. Wow, tonight must have been really good for him to be this pleasant.

He set everything on the table, helped himself and told her to eat. She did, still trying to be dainty about it. This was the best meal she had had in months and she savored every bite. She ate as much as she could without getting sick. Then she sat back and patted her tummy. Her eyes were closed so she didn't see the look on his face as he watched her. So when he reached over and pinched her, hard, she flinched and tears came to her eyes.

"Get on back where you belong and don't expect this every night." he snarled.

She jumped from her seat and was back on her bench as fast as she could. Well, he was true to form, not allowing her to have even small pleasures. She consoled herself that at least she was still alive, which was against all the statistics on kidnapped victims.

In the morning, there was a container of fried chicken and salad in a cooler for her to have for breakfast or lunch and a sack of doughnuts. The bruise from last night's pinch still throbbed on her underarm. No, she needed to keep her anger alive and well. Given any chance at all, she had to try to escape.

Chapter 18

George was searching the internet when he read the headlines for last night in the paper. "Jerry, come look at this. Someone torched the house our friendly Trooper lives in, with him in it and he is in the hospital. Says the doors were blocked, too. You think this is our guy with the macabre gifts?"

"I think we need to beef up security around here. Maybe motion sensor alarms to go with the lights since he obviously can get around the cameras and lights. We need to add more and maybe something super loud. We will all have to remember them, so we don't set them off, ourselves. I am thinking we should do this, today."

"We don't have any appointments this morning, how about we go now?" George asked.

"Sounds good to me, let me get my boots on and lets go." Jerry answered.

Jerry called a local security firm and asked about getting a good security system installed and how long would it take? He was pleased with the response and set it up. Then they were on their way to get a few extras for their own peace of mind.

The first stop was the feed store for a couple of spools of barbed wire and plastic insulators. If an electric fence warned them of a grizzly bear, it should warn them of a possible arsonist.

Then they checked a few more stores and picked up odds and ends that might augment the security system that was being installed.

The security van was pulling in as they arrived home. So they spend the next few hours learning how to secure the house and garage. Then they looked over the trees and bushes around the outside of the house. There would still be a couple of areas where a determined person could access the house, but it would be a lot harder to do so undetected.

Then they started stringing the barbed wire around the perimeter, fastening it to trees and large shrubs with the plastic insulators. Then they placed a large Cat battery and fence charger just inside the garage. There was a solar panel against the garage wall to trickle charge the battery. The charger was for 15 miles of fence and they had a few hundred feet, so it would handle a good sized jolt and the barbs would make sure it was felt. Whether it was a large furry animal or a coverall covered human, they would know they were zapped.

The security company posted notices around the property, so people would know it was covered. The electric fence was a surprise. They did call Pudge and Marky to let them know before they came home.

"So, you guys read about the Trooper, eh? I was getting a bit worried about this place, but it looks like you two have it under control." Pudge said.

Marky spotted the electric fence around the entire back yard. "Is that a barbed wire electric fence?"

They assured him it was.

"Wow that should get anyone's attention. Did you test it out to see how it works?" he asked.

"No, but be my guest. I wouldn't mind getting it tested. It seemed a good idea in theory." Jerry answered.

"Uh, that's okay. I think I will take your word for it. I would rather see our perpetrator get tangled up in it."

Thinking about that made the entire day seem better.

***

He was still in a good mood when he came home the next night. The policeman was in the hospital and even though there was no way to find out his condition, just knowing he was still there was good. He could now concentrate on the other four men. Maybe they needed a little warming up, also. He could torch that place easily enough. Maybe get one or two of them, while he was at it.

He would wait until the coming weekend and see about livening up their lives a bit. They were getting too complaisant. Maybe he should go find another plaything for his game. It had been a while since he played.

He nuked a couple of frozen dinners and slapped hers down on the bench beside her. He locked the door as he went back to the kitchen, ate his, then prepared to go out.

He wanted to scope out some of the bars to see what the clientele was like as it had been a long time since he actually went into a bar. The closest he ever came to getting caught was when he tried to pick up a player from one of the seedier bars in town. Plus, there was always the chance someone might recognize him, later. No, if he went in a bar, he never talked to the women nor did he buy anyone a drink. He bought one beer, pretended to drink it for a couple of hours while watching the people to get an idea of who came and went.

He always left a hat on and sat in far corners, looking over the room without appearing to, too much. He never wanted anyone to remember him for any reason.

He started his search that evening. There are numerous seedy little bars around Fairbanks and even some of the not quite so seedy ones had the right clientele.

He watched one group for quite a while and daydreamed about catching them all, together. He could really have a time with four women at once at his mercy. Maybe similar to bird hunting. He found himself almost chuckling and left the bar. No reason to make folks think he was crazy, while he was hunting. One of the women followed him out and would have been easy to take home, but he would have been remembered, and would not take the chance.

This was getting harder to pull off without leaving evidence. He was going to have to start reading up more on forensics so he could tailor his games better. Maybe he should start picking up bags of old clothes at the dump sites and using them to mix hair and fiber samples. He could really add some interest into the game.

When he got home, he didn't seem in a bad or good mood, so she was very careful not to set him off. He still kicked her as she was crawling into her kennel. Her sore face scraped along the wires on the side of the kennel but she did not make a noise. He stooped down to look at her and smiled. That made her blood run cold. What was he planning now?

The fear in her eyes from his unexpected action put him in a good mood as he prepared for bed. Yes, he would plan something even better than usual to make the next one special.

He started looking for used clothing that looked unwashed when he dropped off trash at the transfer site. He picked up a few items and stored them in plastic bags in the back seat of his truck. Knit hats and scarves were good items to keep. Lots of hair and fibers. Even pet beds yielded hairs and fibers and were stuffed in with the hats. He would give them so much evidence they would not know what to be looking for. It would look like an entire commune of people were involved in each game.

Now that he had a supply of evidence on hand, he started hunting in earnest for his next player. He was out almost every evening, looking. He was being picky this time. Everything had to be just so for his new twist to the game. So when he finally found the one he wanted, she appeared to be just waiting for him.

He stopped and asked her if she needed a ride and she accepted. He played the gentleman and came around and opened the door for her. Then he helped her fasten her seat belt, talking about safety first. She didn't know until she attempted to unlock the seatbelt, that it was not going to open for her. She found that out when he turned the wrong way at the second stop. Then she found the door handle was removed on the inside on the passenger door. Right after that, she found the window control didn't work on her side, either.

Up until that point, she had not panicked. Now, she went into full panic mode. She started screaming and pounding on the dash and window, hoping someone would notice. When she turned toward him, he punched her in the face as hard as he could. Her head ricocheted off the side window and she slumped forward in her seat, only held up by the seatbelt.

She was still slumped over as he pulled into his yard and behind the house. He unlocked the shed and turned up the heat. Then he opened the passenger door and unlocked her seatbelt. She slid out and he caught her as she fell to the ground. He carried her into the shed, closing and locking the door behind him.

He placed her on the bed and started stripping off her clothes. Once everything was removed, he tied her to the bed and taped her eyes and loosely gagged her mouth. Looking at her, he figured he broke her jaw when he hit her. She was still breathing, but she was really out of it. He moved the jaw around and it wasn't broken but badly dislocated, so he popped it back in place. He might want it in working order. The bump on the other side of her head from hitting the window was quite the goose egg, but not his concern. So she would have a headache, so what?

He closed up the shed and walked back over to the house. He would check her out better when she was awake. They were not much fun asleep.

He unlocked the doors and sure enough, the girl was where she belonged. He was tired so they went in and she got in her kennel. He didn't even kick or hit her tonight, so she figured he was tired or distracted. Either one worked for her.

He got up early to check on his new plaything before he headed for work. He liked calling them players now, instead of toys. They needed to learn to play their parts better though. Of course, they didn't last long enough to actually get good at what he expected of them.

When he walked in the shed, he saw her trying to get loose from her ties. He slapped her lightly to get her attention and told her no getting loose allowed. He told her if she followed orders and did as she was told, she might be okay when he turned her loose.

Of course he was lying and she probably knew that somewhere deep inside, but right now, she was too afraid to think clearly. He asked if she understood and she nodded her head yes. He said he would take the tape off her eyes then, if she would behave. She held still and he tore the tape off, pulling hair and skin with it and leaving her gasping in pain. Then he undid the gag and she started to open her mouth but he slapped her lightly across the mouth and told her no speaking unless told to speak.

With tears in her eyes, she nodded. Women's voices irritated him and he did not like listening to them, at all. Making a woman be quiet was something he really enjoyed, even when he was hurting them, he did not want to hear any talking or voices.

Good, this one was listening. He helped her drink some water and then retied the gag loosely around her mouth. He needed to leave for work and she would be fine here the rest of the day. Hungry? Yes, she would be and also thirsty again and needing the bathroom, if she managed to wait. If not, he would punish her yet again. It was all part of the game.

All day he looked forward to his evening after he got home. He made plans and then made different plans. He knew even his best plans were subject to change, it all depended on how things went, once he started.

***

Jerry and George stopped over at the hospital each day to see the Trooper until he was released from the hospital. Jerry offered him his last spare bedroom if he wanted to rent it until he had a place to move back into, after he was released.

The man smiled and told him thanks, but since they were part of an ongoing investigation, he really couldn't live in the same house as they were. Not that they were even considered guilty of anything, but it might look bad in Court, if they had to testify and they were sharing a home with a State Trooper that could coach them on their testimony.

He suffered from smoke inhalation and had some fairly serious burns, but would recover fully. Now he was mainly still here because he did not have family in the area and his home was gone. The doctor did not want him overdoing it if he was home on his own.

He really was lucky to have made it out alive. One of the men at work was looking for an apartment for him until he could look for another house or see about getting his rebuilt. This time of year, that wasn't going to happen very soon.

The insurance company wasn't fighting it as owner induced, so he would receive a check for the amount of loss and could rebuild. He thought he might use the money to buy something in another neighborhood and sell the property. He liked the area a bit out of town much better and this would give him the push to move.

Chapter 19

The newspaper had an article about a missing woman, Lorena Turner, on the front page. Her family was offering a nice reward for information.

"Look at this. This happened just last night. Maybe even while we were at the hospital. We drove right by the area where she disappeared." George was so upset he was almost yelling.

Maybe it was while they were driving home. There had been an older pickup pulled over beside the road that they had passed, but neither of them paid any attention to it or the people standing beside it. It just looked like the man was opening the door for the woman to get in.

"Wait a minute. When we were coming home. Do you remember passing the pickup pulled over? Wasn't some man helping a woman get into the truck? Do you remember what they looked like at all or the truck?" Jerry asked.

George thought about it a while. "I think the pickup was an older model and pale yellow or rusty white. It had big homemade bumpers on it."

"That matches the description of the vehicle that hit you, George."

They started writing down everything either one remembered about the vehicle and the people. But since no one was arguing or fighting while they

161

passed, they really had not paid any special attention to the scene. They added what little they had to the poster on the wall. They would mention it to the Trooper when they visited tomorrow evening. Then George asked if they should wait, considering maybe the woman's life was in danger?

Jerry called the hospital and asked to talk to the officer they stopped to see, only to be told he was checking out now and if it was important, they could transfer the call to accounting.

Jerry considered it important, so they transferred the call. The Trooper was surprised to hear from him and at his present location.

"Listen, I didn't want to call in and be told this was stupid and I should have kept quiet. But last night as we were coming home from visiting with you, we saw an older model pickup pulled over beside Goldstream Road and a man was assisting a woman into the truck. I don't know if that is the area that woman disappeared from, or not, but it was an older off white or pale yellow pickup. Homemade large bumpers. It matches the description of the vehicle that hit George. If this isn't important, I am sorry to have bothered you, but figured if a woman's life is at stake, maybe it would help."

"Okay, I am renting a place not all that far from your place. I will come by and get written statements from you both about this and add it to the information at the office. I don't know if it will be important or not, but I will sort it out later after I read the reports. Thanks for calling and I will see you in about an hour."

When the Trooper pulled in, they had some fresh coffee made and were prepared to sit down and fill out papers. He looked at the chart they had made on the poster on the wall and asked if he could have copies of some of it. George made copies while Jerry and the Trooper talked. They had a map of the local area and put marks where each incident occurred. They did not know where the women that were taken were placed on the map, but they had everything else they knew about. The Trooper looked it over carefully and told them they had a good idea going there and if they didn't mind, he would like to come by and check it once in a while.

After the Trooper left, Pudge came in and asked what was up? They explained it all to him, then again, when Marky came home. They figured they should record it and just press play when they were asked.

***

He wanted to see how the officer was doing, so he stopped by the hospital on his way home. When he was told the man had been discharged, he thanked the receptionist and walked back to his pickup. Well, he wasn't hurt all that bad now, was he, if he was already back out and going home. Oh, wait, he didn't have a home, did he? He was practically laughing by the time he reached his truck and decided he better get out of there or he would be locked in the psycho ward for observation. Then his pet and new player would starve. Time to head for home.

When he got home, he checked the shed first and was upset that the fire had gone out in the furnace sometime and the player was practically frozen. The blankets had slid partway off her and she had not been able to pull them back. She was unresponsive and he bundled her in the blankets after untying her and put her on his porch. He really didn't want the pet to see that he had another woman under his control.

He placed her on the floor over near the door, out of the way and fixed a quick meal in the microwave and dropped it on the bench beside Éclair before going back and seeing to the player. He relocked the door between them so she would not attempt coming into the kitchen.

He pushed the door against the player and went out to see to the furnace. Out of oil. Great. Just what he needed, the delivery man must not have noticed there were two tanks to keep filled here. He returned to the house and called the fuel company and bawled them out for not filling both tanks and letting his shop/shed freeze up. The water pipes would all need thawed and probably replaced, if he knew anything at all about plumbing.

When he returned to the house, the new player was still and not moving. She was not going to be any fun for a long time. He bundled her back up and carried her out to the back of his pickup. He drove to the closest transfer site and as it was fairly late in the evening, he had the place to himself. He looked around to make sure, then got out and took the quilt wrapped bundle and dropped her down into a dumpster. She wasn't responsive since the ride in, even when he pinched her.

He would find another one to play with. There were always girls out along the streets and roads. Besides, this one was loaded with extra evidence on the quilt from the items he was collecting from the dump. If she was found, they would have a lot to look at, if she was not found, oh well.

He wasn't feeling too good yet from the flu or whatever it was so decided to just go home and get some sleep.

***

The boy came out from behind the dumpster where he had been hiding, afraid it was his father looking for him when the pickup pulled in. He was shivering and very cold but not ready to listen to the lecture about responsibility and growing up just yet.

He watched the man get out and drag a bundle of quilts from the pickup and throw them into the middle dumpster, then leave. Definitely not his father.

Maybe if he hurried, the blankets would still be warm from in the truck and he could manage to stay gone all night. Then his dad might be so happy to find him alive and well, that he wouldn't get punished. He hated getting grounded.

When he reached in for the quilt, someone moaned and he just about messed himself and screamed like his little sister. "Geez, man, get a grip. You are 14 years old now, not 3. There ain't nothing here that is going to get you."

He reached in again and a very cold hand grasped his arm. He levitated, he knew he did. He screamed some more and was still screaming when the headlights pulled into the transfer station. The car pulled over beside him and a lady asked him if he was okay. His scream was down to a whimper as he pointed into the dumpster and gulped back tears.

The woman grabbed her small bag of trash and came around to see what the problem was, other than an underage boy out by himself in the middle of the night.

She shined her flashlight into the dumpster and joined the boy in his renewed screaming. A pale arm and hand had hold of the boy's arm and it looked as though there was no getting loose from it.

The woman finally grabbed her cell phone and hit 911 and between gulps, told the person that answered that they needed police and ambulance at the Goldstream transfer station as soon as possible.

Finally, she realized there had to be someone attached to that arm and hand and pulled the quilt away enough to see a badly battered face and naked body and speedily covered the woman back up before the boy got even more traumatized. She eased the grip the woman had on the boy's arm and helped him sit in the front seat of her car to wait for the police. Then she took the heavy parka she kept in her car and pulled the quilt back enough to wrap the parka, warm from the car, around the cold woman in the dumpster.

When the police pulled in, the boy started to open his door to make a run for it and the woman told him to stay put. They needed to think of the poor woman in the dumpster more than their own problems right at the moment. The boy settled back in his seat and thought there actually were worse things than having his dad mad at him for a while. Now that he thought about it, he really wanted to see his dad.

"Ma'am? Could I use your phone and call my Dad? He is going to be mad at me but he is also going to be worried and I really need him, right now."

The woman handed him her phone and he called his father. By this time, the man was so worried, he didn't even yell at him before he listened and said he would be right there. The boy closed the phone and handed it back to the woman.

"Thanks, I appreciate that and I am so glad you came. I was really scared."

"I'll be honest with you, there for a couple of minutes, I was really scared, too. I'm really glad no one was around with a camera. We must have looked a sight, hopping around shrieking."

The tap on the window should not have scared them but they both jumped when it happened. The woman stepped out of the car and took the officer over to the dumpster. He shined the light in and jumped back. Then stepped forward and reached in to feel for a pulse.

The woman told him she and the boy didn't know whether it would be better to leave the poor woman where she was or try to pull her out and maybe hurt her even more, so she just put the warm parka over her and tucked it in around her as well as she could.

The ambulance pulled in and the officer motioned the crew over. They quickly assessed the situation and one of the men jumped into the dumpster and carefully lifted the injured woman out to the crew members waiting to assist. The officer bagged everything, including the woman's parka and told her they would need to go over it in case any evidence from the woman's body and blankets were now on the parka. She would get it back, but he didn't know when.

Another pickup pulled into the transfer site and the boy was out of the car, running to it before it even got completely stopped.

"Dad, oh Dad, I am so sorry, I just want to go home."

"Are you okay? Why is there an ambulance and the police here? What happened?"

The woman was standing there, beside her car, watching the boy reunite with his father. She figured they would work out their problems now and maybe both appreciate the other a bit more. She walked over and introduced herself.

"Hi, I'm Janelle Weaver. I just stopped by to drop off trash on my way home and your son and I found a woman in the dumpster. Your son has been a big help and I want to let you know he probably saved her life, if she makes it."

"Thanks, I'm James Mason and this is my son, Jordan. I'm glad he did a good deed, but he and I have some talking to do, as soon as we can go home.

I guess I need to speak to the Officer in charge here."

He walked over to speak to the Officer and Janelle put her arm around Jordan's shoulders.

"You did a good thing, helping find this woman. I would have stopped, thrown the bag in from the back of my car and pulled out. No one would have found her until tomorrow and by then she would not have a chance at all. You gave her a chance to live. Just remember that."

After leaving contact information, they went home.

***

George had not checked the security on their webpage for quite a while. So he was surprised to find that someone still had attempted to hack in again. He traced the IP back, but still didn't know who it could be and why they would bother. A small time politician shouldn't warrant that much effort to hack.

He added the info to the chart and went ahead on making some updates to the website. Most of the comments were still positive. There were always a few soreheads that would complain if they were hung with a new rope.

All in all, the campaign was going quite well. They were getting name recognition, which was important and people were putting up signs in support on their lawns and fences. There were bumper stickers showing up, too. The opponent was the exact opposite of Jerry, so it would be an easy choice for

most voters, he thought. Now just getting them to
see it that way.

Chapter 20

Stupid! He was so stupid! Why didn't he make sure the woman would never survive? He should have taken the time to take her apart and scatter her around a bit or even still use the dumpsters, but to leave her alive and wrapped in a quilt was just plain stupid. He was losing his edge.

The woman had seen him and could give a detailed description to the police. She didn't know where he lived, so that was in his favor. He also had been wearing winter gear and a hat, so maybe she wouldn't know exactly what he looked like. There were just too many unknowns for him to know whether or not he should be moving out or hiding or just continue going to work every day.

He was getting soft. A regular job and a warm house were making him forget the survival instincts that kept him alive and ahead of the game. Now he was making stupid mistakes. He was cleaning up his shed, trying to make sure there were no signs of how it was used. He even took the bed apart and stored the pieces in the small loft. Then he made a small workbench where the bed used to be.

The fuel company delivered fuel last night while he was gone, dumping the woman. He did not want any sign that anyone could find how he usually spent his time out here. They might send someone to assess damage to the plumbing since he made such a big fuss about it on the phone.

Sure enough, a van pulled in from a plumbing contractor as he was stepping out the door of the shed. He motioned the man back and they went in. The plumber looked over the small bathroom and agreed it would need totally redone. The water was turned off already so he took measurements and made plans on when he could return and repair the bathroom. He said he could do it on the weekends, if needed. They agreed on starting the following weekend and he left.

The girl was so scared. She knew something was wrong when the man came back, last night. He was so angry that he punched her, which he seldom did. Usually he only slapped her around. She thought she might have a broken rib but was afraid to react when he looked at her or touched her. She thought he was just looking for an excuse to get rid of her now.

Shortly after she arrived, she had started doing isometric exercises to try and keep some muscle tone. She was afraid if the chance to escape ever did appear that she would be too weak to have any chance at all. Sitting on a bench most of the time or laying in a kennel did nothing to keep any muscle. She now started the isometric exercises as soon as he left and didn't stop until all her muscles burned and she was exhausted. As soon as she recovered a bit, she went right back to it. She thought she just might be a bit stronger now than she was when he caught her. The rib was bothering her, but after a while, she decided it probably was only badly bruised.

She heard him rummaging around in the kitchen, so held very still, on her bench. She knew he would look at the monitor once in a while to make sure she was still where she was supposed to be. The days he stayed around the house were very hard for her to manage a bathroom break without him catching her off her bench. Then he punished her.

***

As usual, George was the first one to read the news about the woman being found. While the others got ready for work or just got around for breakfast, he usually checked the headlines on-line.

"Hey guys, that woman, Lorena Turner, that was taken the other night has been found, alive." he yelled.

Everyone clustered into his room to read the news over his shoulder. The news was very sketchy about details, but did say she was in the hospital and in guarded condition, whatever that meant. No mention was made of the boy that found her.

"If they have any sense, it means they have guards around her, to keep her alive. Whoever had her is not going to be all that happy to find out she is still alive."

"I don't think that is exactly what they mean, but that would be a very good idea, anyway."

Pudge and Marky still needed to get to work, so left George and Jerry to mull over the article and wonder why this one was left alive and in one piece. They added her information to their chart.

"We should ask that guard at the Pump Station what he did with our information, Jerry."

"I've been thinking about that, too. Want to go on a road trip?"

"Sure, we could be back before the guys even get home."

Jerry started his pickup and they were soon on their way.

"We could have had breakfast at the truck stop. Oh well, maybe an early lunch?" They both laughed.

When they passed their usual camping area, they looked sadly at the mounds of snow blocking the old road access.

"Do you think we will ever camp there again? I don't think it would be the same, after this last season." Jerry said.

"I don't know. I would probably always think of finding that bag, myself. But maybe we should, to erase the bad memories. Let's see, next moose season."

As they pulled up to the Guard Shack, a different Guard came out to see what they wanted. They explained what they were wanting and he laughed.

"Yeah, we all heard about you guys finding a bag of trash and thinking it was a body. Pretty dumb to try making up something like that. Didn't you think we have to go check before we turn anything in and embarrass the company for a false report? You are lucky he didn't go ahead and turn you in for that. There is a pretty good fine for that, you know."

"We just want to know what happened to the report we made here and our contact information."

"Oh, we burned it all. We have our own trash system here and all paper goods are burned. We had a good laugh over that, as we threw the papers on the burn pile."

"Who all got to see the papers before you burned them?"

"Just about everyone here at the Station. We don't get many laughs on this job, so we all share the ones we get."

"Okay, thanks for your time. What was the Guard's name that we talked to?"

"Oh, that was old Art. He thinks he fools all of us by dying his hair, but he is a lot older than he put down on his paperwork when he was hired."

"What's old Art's last name?"

"Well, I'm probably not supposed to tell you, but what can it hurt? Art Jamison."

"Thank you and we appreciate you talking to us."

"You are welcome. This is a pretty boring job and we need all the entertainment we can get. You guys supplied us with laughs for several days."

They both mulled over the information they had just received as they headed back to town.

"So. Anyone at the Pump Station could be our Stalker?"

"Sure sounds that way. If they all saw the paperwork, anyone there could have decided to play games with us by adding us to the other macabre game he plays. But I am pretty sure now it has to be a man."

"Yes, it would have taken a very strong woman to lift that woman wrapped in quilts into the dumpster."

"I wasn't just thinking of that. The Guard never mentioned anything but the guys. I think he would have added if there were any women on the payroll."

***

Well, if he couldn't go find another toy, he would just see about torching the men in their house one of these nights. He had plenty of containers and old rags to use, even for that large house. He would start stockpiling them tonight, full of gasoline, back in the trees just behind the motion sensors.

He was feeling pretty good with his plan when he hit the barbed wire fence. The 12 volt battery and large charger sent a really good jolt through the barbs that pierced his outer pants into his flesh. He was not proud of the screams he let loose before he caught himself.

To make matters worse, he managed to get tangled in the wire so it was jolting him into a jerky dance he could not control. Each new piercing by the barbs tore into him with jolts that made him jerk around uncontrollably. He finally tore loose and made it back to his pickup, parked on a small access road on the other side of the stand of trees.

What the hell had just happened and what evil Mind would think up something like that? He thought he was good at thinking up ways to get people, but that was just plain diabolical.

He got the truck out to the main road and headed for home. His legs were torn and bleeding through his insulated pants. He was going to have a time patching up this mess and hated to see what it looked like under the pants legs that hung in shreds from his waist.

By the time he pulled into his yard, he could barely hobble. Most of the bleeding seemed to have stopped, but he knew when he pulled the material away from the cuts, that most would start up again. This was worse than getting cut by a razor. They at least made a clean cut that didn't hurt that bad at the moment, just later, after the body caught up with the sharp slice.

His legs looked even worse than he thought they would. The punctures and tears were jagged and oozing. He sat in his kitchen, wishing the shed was repaired and he could use the shower in there. He hated getting blood in the bathroom in his house.

The girl was locked in her kennel, so he didn't have to see her eyes, trying to look sorry but gloating over his pain. If he saw that in her face, she would be gone in seconds and then he would not get the pleasure of making it a lingering death. No, it was better if he doctored himself and left her in the kennel, unaware of his injuries.

***

By the time they located the area where the screams were coming from, the instigator was long gone. The evidence remained though. There would be plenty of tissue and blood samples for the police lab to work with.

They called the police and soon there were a couple of cars and a van in their yard. One used a light and followed the trail left by the person involved out to the side access road and took pictures of the tracks. There really wasn't anything they could do about tire tracks in snow, but it was procedure.

They found the containers of gasoline set out in the trees and the ones dropped at the scene of the fence encounter.

"Looks like you were supposed to be the main event at a roast, tonight, Jerry." the Officer said.

"Yes and I am just as glad not to have the honor. You didn't seem to enjoy it at all. When you have some spare time, George and I went out and talked to a Guard at the Pump Station. We didn't learn much, except they are still of the opinion that we filed a false claim and are telling everyone that."

"Okay, we planned on doing some background checks there, and never got it followed up on. The reports should be somewhere in the office. I need to look into that, later today. Maybe we can let them know it wasn't a false report, so no one thinks that is something to use against you in your campaign."

"Thanks, I would appreciate that. I've tried not to think it would be a big deal, but my opponent would try to make it a big deal."

"Okay, that is the least I can do. You have been a help. Off the record, of course."

"Of course."

Chapter 21

He was hurting and she was thinking that she better come up with some idea for escape while he was not as able to catch her. She still wasn't too sure exactly how she could manage it, but she had to make the move. The way he was looking at her now, she figured he was planning on how he was going to get rid of her and she would rather leave on her own without it hurting or killing her.

He was not locking all the doors as it required him to turn and stand longer on his aching legs. When he got healed up, he was truly going to make it his life's ambition to get all four of those men. They would pay and pay big time for this.

She watched and waited, looking for her chance. While in the bathroom, he barged in and slapped her. She fell back against the toilet and the lid on the tank clattered.

Later, she thought about that sound and realized that lid was the largest, most solid item she had around to use. She knew he was preoccupied with his thoughts which looked dark indeed. He scowled all the time now and the look in his eyes was frightening. She had not been this afraid of him in months.

Her bench was now fairly close to the door that he always used. He was seldom locking it or the outside door as he was in and out a lot. He must have either taken time off work or gotten fired as he never left during the day now and seldom at night.

Whatever had happened to his legs was consuming him with hatred. His mutterings to himself filled her with fear. He mixed up past, present and future in his ramblings and she didn't know what had already happened, what he was planning for immediately or what he wanted to do in the future.

She continued her isometric exercises and thought she was in fairly good condition now. Her rib still hurt, but she was sure it was bruised, maybe cracked, but not broken.

He was not giving her food very often and she thought he was not eating either. His eyes were getting a pale yellow color to them that did not look healthy. She would have to make a move soon or she would be too weak to follow through on it.

***

Jerry was glad to hear the woman in the hospital would survive. She was suffering from some frostbite, but would keep all her fingers, toes and face. She would lose some skin and it would be painful for quite a while. Frostbite is similar to being burned and the treatments are about the same, once the flesh is thawed. It is very painful, but she was just happy to be alive.

She gave the police a detailed description of the man that abducted her and the composite drawing was a fairly good rendition of him. His picture was being plastered all over the papers, TV and bulletin boards around town. The boy that found her described the pickup in great detail. The description was on all the posters of the man. It was now only a matter of time.

Jerry, Pudge and Marky restrung the wire that was pulled loose the night the intruder woke them all up. They knew a moose might wander into it now and then, but it gave them some peace of mind, knowing it did its job. They doubted if the man would try coming back again, this way, but they didn't want to take chances.

The snow was melting and daylight hours increasing enough that they could post some more cameras around the place. They found a great deal at a warehouse store on monitoring cameras for security and bought the set with 6 cameras and recording capabilities.

***

He was still ill, but she thought his legs were getting better. She finally caught a glimpse of them one evening from her kennel and almost gagged. The flesh was torn and shredded and he had not managed to close all the gashes with butterfly bandages. His legs looked terrible. But if they were healing, she needed to take her chance and get out of here. One try would be all she would get. She knew she would not be able to by the next weekend. He was making plans for her that scared her to death. She managed to move her sharp pieces of wire into the living room she was kept in. She didn't know if she could manage to use them for anything, but they gave her confidence. She started keeping at least one tucked into her long hair.

While he was out of the house, she scooted the bench a little bit closer to the door. Then she brought the lid from the toilet tank into the living room, also. She listened for his steps by the kitchen door and hopped up on the bench, bringing the tank lid with her.

As he opened the door from the kitchen, she brought the lid back behind her head and as he stepped through, she swung, with all her might.

He caught movement from the corner of his eye and started to turn toward it just as the lid hit him across the face. The lid shattered, taking out one eye and most of his nose. The other eye was smashed under the remains of his nose and cheekbones. He fell to the floor and she was right on top of him, stabbing as many times and she could, with the sharp heavy wire and the remains of the tank lid...

She jumped off him and ran into the kitchen, turning on the propane stove as she went by it, then grabbing the bottle of cooking oil on the counter and spraying it all over the stove top, the counter and floors. Flames soared up along the trail of oil and she grabbed his coat off the hanger by the door and went right on out the door.

She heard screaming behind her, but she did not slow down until she had to decide which way led to the main road. She kept running as she tried to cover her bare body with the large coat. Her feet were sore, but so what? She was free. She ran as long as she could, gasping for breath and fighting the stitch in her side. Even when she collapsed, her legs kept trying to run.

The hands that picked her up seemed gentle and she sighed. She was safe. Then her eyes flew open and she started screaming. A woman's voice broke through her panic and she stopped screaming. She reopened one eye and saw that the man that had picked her up and sat her in their car was not the one she was running from. He was looking rather spooked, himself, from her reaction to him.

"Oh please, we have to leave. If he catches us, we are all in danger." she pleaded in her rusty unused voice.

"Okay, Missy, we are on our way. You going to be okay until we get to town?" the man asked.

She nodded her head yes and they closed the doors and pulled out onto the highway. The woman kept murmuring softly to her, as though she were an injured child but it was soothing and calmed her down.

When they got in cell range, the woman called the police. She spoke to someone and said they were headed to the hospital. She gave directions to where they had picked up the girl and was assured a Trooper would be in that area, looking for evidence in a very short while. As they were speaking, a police car passed them, headed the way they just came from.

Soon, another one did, also. Then a third one. They were definitely taking this seriously.

As they pulled into emergency unloading for the hospital, George and Jerry were coming out the door from visiting with the woman found at the dump, Lorena Turner. They were looking for any information she might remember, no matter how miniscule, that might give them a lead. Jerry hurried over to help, but the young woman recoiled back from him. George rolled up in his wheelchair that he still used for long term visiting and town.

"Hey there, you okay? What's your name? " he asked her softly.

She looked at him, and something seemed to mesh in her mind. Maybe it was the wheelchair, but he did not scare her. She had to think a moment, then told him her name, "Suzy, my name is Suzy Dennison. I'm not a pet or Éclair." Everyone around looked oddly at her, but she didn't care. She was alive, she was safe and she was herself again. She had her name back. She smiled a very small smile and walked beside him into the hospital. An Officer pulled up as they went inside and hurried to take charge.

When a hospital worker attempted to take the large coat she was wrapped in, she would not let go. Her long hair partially covered her, but not enough. George thought he understood and asked a nurse if they had a gown that the woman could use. The young woman nodded agreement. Somehow, something about George calmed her down.

Jerry stayed back and talked to the couple that brought her in. Then another Officer pulled up and joined then. Jerry stepped back, but listened in. They told about seeing her running slowly along the highway, in obvious distress and still trying to run, even after she fell and could no longer move.

She was covered with old and new bruises, with a lot of dried blood all over her. The first nurse that saw her bare body stepped into the hallway, and looked out the door toward George in the lobby, as though she was going to personally hang him. George caught the look and tried to look innocent.

The young woman asked what day and date it was, which the nurse thought was strange. The nurse told her and she moaned softly.

"I have been a prisoner for almost 7 months. What will my family be thinking?"

The nurse looked at her in surprise. Then looked her over more closely. The damaged cheekbone and the slightly crooked nose told of older injuries than the recent bruising all over the woman. As she helped clean her up, none of the blood seemed to have come from her and the Officer was bagging everything, keeping samples.

She felt like she was being vacuum cleaned, they were so thorough. Everything would be used as evidence.

***

The house was going to be a complete loss. He was trying to see out of his remaining eye and just felt lucky to have escaped when he did. He found his bag of movies and photos in the shed and stuck them behind the seat after he found his newer pickup. It was going to be a chore to drive, with his ruined face. The lack of depth perception was the worst part. If he found that bitch, he was going to run over her, back up and run over her again and again.

He should have learned, years ago. If they escape, they will go get the Troopers onto your case. He didn't have much money here, on him, and anything that was in the house was gone. He couldn't just walk into his bank, looking like this. She had really messed him up and after he was so good to her, too. That was just like a woman. No gratitude. He would make sure the next one learned her lessons better and permanently. But first, he wanted to find this one.

He made it out onto the main highway and then pulled over at the first pullout to try and clean up his face a bit.

Then he saw the police car go by, followed quickly be two more. What? She got them on him already? At least few knew about this pickup and the other one was still at the remains of the burning house.

He covered his missing eye and half his nose with a clean folded handkerchief and taped the edges with small bits of duct tape. Maybe he could walk in one of the Urgent Care facilities and say he was falling a tree and it barber chaired into his face.

He drove slowly into town and pulled into the first place he saw and carefully parked his truck. The receptionist behind the counter gasped when she looked at his face. He tried to smile and asked if he could see someone about getting sewed together. She handed him a pile of papers to fill out while she went back to find someone.

He was having trouble reading the papers without reading glasses or both eyes. When she came back in, he asked if she would help him fill them out as he was having trouble seeing. She did and soon a nurse came up to see what was needed. She took him directly back and removed the temporary bandage he put over it and looked at the wreckage that had been his face.

"Wow, you really did it up good. You really should be at the hospital. What happened?"

"I was falling some trees for firewood and one barber chaired on me. This place is closest and I just need sewed up."

"What's barber chaired?"

"When you cut partway through the tree and it starts to fall but splits partway up and the cut through part swings out leaving part of the tree attached and the rest hanging out like a barber chair. It's hard to talk, you know? Can we get this fixed up?"

When the nurse came back in, she told him he was in luck today, an actual doctor was here and had some time free. He would be in, in a few minutes. She gave him some shots to locally deaden the pain in his face for the ordeal that was ahead yet.

The doctor breezed in the door a few minutes later saying, "I hear we have some sewing to do in here. Sounds like it impressed the nurses."

Then he got a good look at the face watching him and faltered a step. "Oh my, guess we do, at that. I can do it, but you would be more comfortable at the hospital."

"What, so I can sit and wait in the waiting room while all the drunks and possible heart attacks get taken care of first? No thanks, Doc, just sew me up."

He swayed a bit on the bench as the doctor tried to push his nose back into place a bit more. Even with the shots, that hurt. The doctor applied some tape over the bridge of his nose and told him he couldn't totally repair it as it seemed maybe some bits were missing. The eye on that side was completely gone and nothing to be done for it. He could clean out the socket and later a glass eye could be used or he could just sew it shut for him. He opted for sewing it shut. He would wear a patch over it.

The doctor spent quite a while, piecing his face back together. He would certainly never win any beauty pageants with the face he had now. Nor could he count on being anonymous. Anyone that saw him from now on, would remember him.

By the time the doctor was finished and the nurse had bandaged him back up, he was feeling decidedly woozy. He figured he better go find some place he could sleep a while.

He started up his pickup and heard someone tapping on his window. He turned his head to look and saw the younger of the two nurses standing outside his truck.

"Sir, you should not drive. I am just getting off shift and can drive you where you need to go, if you wait a couple of minutes."

Ha, he thought, so you want to go with me. You can get us out of town then I'll take over and you will be my next toy.

He was smiling a little as she came over and got in his pickup. She asked which way he wanted to go. He asked if out towards Nenana would be too far out of the way for her. She laughed and said she lived out that direction and started out.

He saw a side road that looked plowed but not well used ahead and asked if she would pull in, he needed to relieve himself. She obliged. He walked over into the edge of the bushes and while he was there, went ahead and did relive himself. Then he pretended to stagger a bit and lean against the tree he was standing beside. She rushed over to help him and he let her help him back toward the truck. As they reached the front of the truck, he punched her. Then as she opened her mouth in shock, he punched her again and caught her before she hit the ground.

He half carried her around to the driver's side and opened the back door, plopping her onto the small back seat. Then he tied her hands and feet together so she couldn't kick at him if she came to and taped her mouth and eyes. He checked her purse and found a credit card and quite a bit of cash. He kept the card and cash and threw the purse over the bank.

He was feeling pretty good when he got back in the driver's seat and headed out to the main road. Then he changed directions and headed back toward Fairbanks.

In Ester, he filled both tanks on the pickup on the credit card, then left it in the trash. He started to go on into town, then decided to go over Goldstream Road and maybe head towards Circle. There were a lot of side roads he could check out up that way. He could play with his new toy a bit, then come back this way and go on down toward Anchorage and get lost in the population down there.

When he stopped at the intersection in Fox, he changed his mind yet again and started to turn towards Livengood. The tractor trailer rig was almost on him and he had not seen it at all out of his ruined eye and could barely see it from the other. He floored the accelerator and the tractor barely grazed his back bumper, the horn was blaring on the big rig and he understood he almost wiped out, right there.

He drove a bit farther and pulled over to catch his breath on that one. Too close. Then he started out again, driving with more care.

Chapter 22

The road he wanted was still piled high with snow. Now what? He pulled back onto the main road and drove on a bit farther. Another side road and it also was too deeply drifted to attempt to drive on. Snow was melting fairly well in town, but out here, it was still too deep to get off the main right of way.

He passed the Pump Station and saluted the road as he passed. He knew there were no side roads off that one and it was fairly well traveled.

He thought of taking the old road right of way next, but it looked blocked a bit farther down, with deep snow. When he came to the large gravel pit with the high gravel pile in it, he saw that the snow was plowed around behind it, so he turned in. When he parked just so, behind it, his pickup was not visible from the main road. Okay, maybe time for some fun and games.

While he was cutting her clothes off, she did not excite him like he expected, so he just proceeded to start dismembering her. Maybe it was the anesthetic wearing off, his face hurt.

It was very messy work, with her heart still beating, so he made sure nothing sprayed on the truck. He had a change of clothes for himself in the truck, he always traveled prepared. He should have been a scout, usually prepared.

He was still chuckling over that when he heard a vehicle on the main road. He stayed crouched down behind his truck with the handgun from the pocket in the front of his seat in his hand until the vehicle passed on by. Then it was back to work.

There was a shot up vehicle parked back there, too, so he artfully arranged pieces around in the front seat. This might be his last masterpiece for a while, he wanted it to be perfect.

When he was done, he used some snow to wipe himself off as well as he could, then changed his clothes and wadded the bloody ones up with hers and put them all in a plastic bag with the surgical gloves he always used. He would drop them off at the transfer site on his way back through town.

He stopped at the transfer site and dropped the bags in several dumpsters. As he was getting into his pickup, he heard an excited young man's voice yelling "Dad, Dad, that's the man that threw away the lady."

Well, hell. That blew it. He tried to hurry, opening his pickup door but missed with his bad depth perception and stumbled. Someone drove their vehicle across the exit gate. Then he heard someone on a cell phone yelling for the 911 operator to get the police out here, right now. He finally got his door open and reached in the get the pistol. Something smacked into the door, slamming it on his arm.

He turned his head to look, and someone grabbed his other arm and held it behind his back.

"Easy, Mister. The police are on their way and you can talk it over with them after they get here."

He tried to twist away and the pain from the arm still caught in the door and the arm behind his back almost made him pass out. He slightly turned to ease the pressure on both arms and heard a siren coming and renewed his attempts to get lose.

"Not happening, Bud. Just hold still. If this is a mistake, they will let you go in a little bit. But my son says he saw you put a woman in the dumpster and I believe him."

The young man had found a can of spray paint and was going to each of the dumpsters he had used and marked each one.

"Hey, Kid, what do you think you are doing?" he yelled.

"I saw which ones you used and want to let the Officers check them out. I don't want to miss one." He continued walking and marking.

The vehicle pulled away from the gate to let the Troopers in and soon they had him restrained and in the backseat of one of the cars. He was read his Rights and told them he knew them better than they did.

One of the Troopers was fishing something out of one of the marked dumpsters and when he pulled it over the edge, the bag tore and a leg fell out on the ground.

James Mason grabbed his son and turned him away from the scene. He asked one of the Troopers if he could take his son and go home now.   Since they already had his information, they let them leave.

"Son, I think we will start going to the transfer site near Farmers Loop. This one is too weird."

Jordan agreed with his Dad. "Yes, but Dad, maybe we did a good thing today."

"You certainly did, pointing him out, helping restrain him and marking the dumpsters, you did a very good job and I am proud of you."

"Thanks Dad. You were pretty awesome yourself, grabbing him and holding him until the police got there. He won't hurt anyone ever again, will he?"

"I certainly hope not, Son."

***

"Hey, Guys, I think they caught the man that has been leaving us presents. The kid that found the lady in the dump recognized him again, there, today. They helped apprehend him and he is now sitting in jail, downtown" George read from his screen.

"The young man said there were several plastic bags with more pieces of someone in them, at the dump. He saw which ones the man used and marked them all for the police."

"Hope the boy don't have nightmares from this. That had to be scary, seeing that."

"Well, maybe we can relax a bit now, not having to worry about opening a door or car and having something waiting for us."

"I think we will leave the security measures in place for the time being, I feel better knowing they are there."

"I think we all do. It is easy to get complaisant but this points out that we are all vulnerable in one way or another. We will leave the security in place for now."

***

The Trooper that pulled the bag of pictures and video out from behind the seat of the pickup about lost it when he looked at one of the pictures. He yelled for someone to come look and soon everyone was gathered around the pickup.

They gathered around a table and spread the contents of the bag out to look through. Everything was being tagged and bagged to keep the chain of evidence unbroken. Before this bag was found, they may have only been able to convict on kidnapping charges, but with this evidence, they could go for Murder One. This, plus the evidence of the young man and his father seeing the man dropping the bags of body parts in the dumpsters.

They reached the burned home before the plumber showed up and he stopped at the crime scene tape to see what was happening.

"We want to check the drains. We are looking for tissue and other samples. You can go ahead after we are done although the man that was living here is in jail so I don't know whether or not you will get paid. You might want to check before working."

"I was wondering when I saw the burned house. Nothing has been done since it caught fire." the plumber said. "I think I will go back to town and write it off as a wasted trip. You can go ahead and do whatever you need to do."

When they opened the drains, they found various tissue samples in the trap. They bagged everything for the lab to check out.

When they found the mattress, they looked it over and found some rusty looking spots along the edges and sides. It ended up being blood from several different sources and tied this location to several of the missing women.

***

When George saw the picture of the man on the internet he yelled for the others to come look. He filled the screen with the man's face and they all recognized the Guard from the Pump Station.

So, they had found his stash, reported it to him, he moved it and turned in a bag of trash and a car seat, saying that was what they found, then ridiculed them for making a false report and shared it with the other guards at the Station. When they saw pictures of his old pickup, they remembered seeing it go past them before they turned out onto the road to go report the finding of the body. So it probably was him they saw as a large dark shadow back in the trees in some of their photos. No wonder he stalked them. Suddenly they all felt very lucky to just be alive.

The man not only knew their faces, he had all of their contact information from their driver's licenses and they handed them right over to him. Then they read farther down the report and found he listed himself as a Retired Arsonist. Oh, man. They were so lucky to still be alive, so was the Trooper he targeted. The man was a lifelong bundle of hate and misery.

George got busy doing research on the man and reached a certain point then nothing. It was like he suddenly appeared as a young adult with only a birth showing before that. No parents when searched beyond the birth record.

"Hmmm, looks like someone set up their own identity on here and didn't think to go back farther to set the stage for it. Maybe I should also check for crimes, using the same criteria as this jerk." He went back to researching.

"Do you want to go to the initial hearing? We've sort of been involved from the first, in a round-about way." George asked the rest at breakfast.

"I would rather never see the man ever again," Pudge said. Marky agreed.

"I'll go with you, George, if you really want to go, but I don't want to go to all the hearings and trials that will be held." Jerry offered.

"No, I only want to go and maybe see how that poor girl I talked to at the hospital is doing. I didn't think I was going to get out of there without getting arrested once that nurse decided I was the one responsible for the bruises and other injuries that girl had. I want to see if she is doing okay."

"Once the nurse started in on you, the girl jumped right into it, defending you. She left no doubt that you were not responsible and to leave you alone, you were doing a good deed. After all she has been through, she still has a lot of spark left to her and she is probably doing okay. But yes, it would be nice to see her under different circumstances."

"Does anyone know how the half frozen woman is doing?"

"No, haven't heard or read a thing. I don't think anything has been in the news beyond the initial report."

Later that day, they entered the Courtroom to find several small groups of people sitting around in family groups. Jerry was afraid they represented the families of victims of this monster at the Hearing today. He hoped they all got answers but he was afraid they would not get peace from those answers. He doubted if he would feel any better if he saw pictures of his loved one in the condition he heard most of these were in.

George spotted Suzy Dennison as soon as he got into the room and found himself heading over toward her. He was using his crutches today as it was hard to maneuver a wheelchair in the Courtroom. She looked apprehensive at first but soon recognized him as the man she first felt comfortable with at the hospital. He invited her over to sit with them, as she had no one with her in the room. She accepted and they sat together through the proceedings.

When the prisoner was brought in, he looked at her and smiled. She shrank back in her seat and wished she had not come.

George whispered to her, "He can't hurt you ever again and he is on that side of the rail, never to be free again and you are free to do whatever you want to do and go wherever you want to go. You have won."

Then the Trooper they had been dealing with, testified and brought out the fake identity being used by the prisoner.

His real name was John Thomas Hughes and he was supposed to be doing Life plus 20 years for his crimes several years ago. He had been moved from prison to prison over the years and somehow through a computer glitch, he not only came up for parole, it was granted. Then his records were changed to his being deceased, there were going to be some hard questions asked at assorted prisons.

After finding how easily he had set up a new identity complete with his own fingerprints, allowing him to get a job in security, more changes were due to be made.

As they all filed out, no one was satisfied with the results except that all bail was denied. George offered lunch to the young woman and she accepted. They did tell her their favorite place to eat was the truck stop up the Elliott. She clapped her hands together, "Oh, I love eating there. I will drive up and meet you there. It's on my way home."

They had a great lunch and it helped put them all in better moods. She and George enjoyed seeing each other again and exchanged phone numbers.

***

He was in the shower and did not hear anyone come in, over the sound of the running water. The arm went around his throat and the voice in his ear whispered to him, "This is for my sister." Then the razor sharp blade sliced through his abdomen and again, an X incision, spilling his insides all over the floor. The agony was indescribable. He tried getting away from the arm, his hands frantically attempting to push his insides back in. Then the sharp blade sliced against his jugular, not enough to stop the pain, but deep enough. He dropped into the water, swirling in red around the feet standing behind him, watching him bleed out. He tried to speak, to explain, it was only a game. The attack had only taken seconds.

"See you in Hell, you rotten Son of a Bitch."

www.ingramcontent.com/pod-product-compliance
Lightning Source LLC
Chambersburg PA
CBHW060643260626
47161CB00008B/2978